SECRETS IN THE SKY

Suzanne Parsons

SAPERE
BOOKS

SECRETS IN THE SKY

Published by Sapere Books.

24 Trafalgar Road, Ilkley, LS29 8HH

saperebooks.com

ISBN: 978-0-85495-353-0

PROLOGUE

3rd October 1918

At twelve thousand feet the air thinned rapidly. He felt the familiar light-headedness and the numbness in his extremities. He was glad to be on lone patrol; formations were risky with all the new pilots coming out of Blighty, most of whom could barely fly.

Ascending another few thousand feet and scanning the horizon, he decided to head northwest towards Fricourt. After all, he did have a full tank of fuel.

And then something joined him from behind the sun: in his mirror he spied a dark dot speeding towards his tail.

His safest options were to change direction and make for the Allied lines, or run for home. But instead, he side-winged right, turning his S.E.5a to face the navy Fokker D.VII, and saw to his horror eight more navy dots emerging from behind the sun. Barely visible and strewn above the horizon, they were hurtling towards him at great speed.

Licking his lips as he dodged bullets from the Fokker, he twisted and turned and side-slipped out of its way. No time to think, he grabbed his Lewis gun and fired directly at the lead Fokker's wingtips. It hiccupped, lost height, then steadied itself, rushing at him again, three other triplanes right on his tail. It was time to find out whose nerves could hold the longest.

He lowered his head, kicked his rudder bar, and manoeuvred his S.E.5a so it was heading straight at the leader. He released more bullets from behind even as the lead triplane continued on its course towards him, until — with about thirty feet to spare — the pilot lost his nerve, pulling his nose up in the nick of time. He smiled at this small victory, then heard an unnatural, deafening noise behind him: a clanking, whooshing sound he'd never heard before, and he'd flown at one hundred and twenty miles per hour many a time.

The joystick became rubbery and unresponsive.

He grabbed it hard, swinging it forwards then backwards in an attempt to regain control.

Despite his efforts, the plane started sliding backwards and down, and from the corner of his eye he saw the looming dark, navy shape coming at him again. He needed to put his plane into a tailspin if he was going to get out of this — never his manoeuvre of choice unless absolutely necessary, as it was now. He spiralled his plane towards the earth, but to his surprise found he wasn't alone… The Fokker was following him down.

Affording himself another smile, he heard a whisper in his ear: *Never, ever follow your prey all the way down.*

He grabbed his revolver, firing blindly at the triplane — it hit well, huge black plumes engulfing it. But his own cockpit was becoming hotter now, and the earth was looming ever closer. The heat was searing, and thick, acrid smoke billowed outwards making his eyes stream.

There was only one option.

His hands shook as he lifted the revolver.

He thought of Ayda.

I'm sorry. So sorry.

He thought of his friends already departed for their castles in the air.

The Fokker exploded below him. He closed his eyes, lifted the barrel against his temple, and fired.

PART 1

CHAPTER 1

September 1912, Hertfordshire, England

Sixteen-year-old Ayda de Corsi looked at the muddy meadows, at the oak and ash trees in the golden pastures, marvelling at her new home. The scent of earth and grass made her nose twitch as she inspected her surroundings — a long way from her birthplace in Italy, and much grander than the other places her nomadic mother had taken her to in England. Their arrival a few weeks ago at Lord Bound's Aldenham estate in Hertfordshire, had promised much: a position for Rosina and a chance of a better life for Ayda.

Ayda had barely left the cottage since the move, stuck indoors while her mother worked long hours. She had briefly been introduced to Lord Bound when they had first arrived — an intimidating, imposing man — but she hadn't yet met the rest of his family. Now that the rain had finally stopped, she had decided to venture out and explore the grounds.

The cooing call of a cuckoo led her to a grey stone barn. The barn doors were open and she crept inside. Her heart missed a beat. Books lay piled almost to the rafters: thin ones, thick ones, colourful ones, weighty ones, worn ones drawing her in, speaking to her — take me, open me, read me, *learn* from me.

Up to now, Ayda's education had been snatched between moves, but she loved learning, and she found she picked things up with ease, especially numbers which she seemed to have a natural affinity with. Ayda had scanned ledgers from a young age, easily calculating the totals in her mind. Rosina hadn't seemed to understand the value of numbers and books, and she hadn't encouraged Ayda in her learning, though she was adamant Ayda would not end up like her, forced into a life of drudgery.

Ayda looked around at the towers of books in front of her. She would give anything to have access to a library full of books such as these. Books promised knowledge, adventure, and something solid Ayda could hold in the palm of her hand.

She remembered the day she had first seen a book. Aged three or four, newly arrived in Merseyside, she saw a pedlar at the dockside selling books of all shapes and sizes from an old wheelbarrow. Opening one, his thin lips had wrapped themselves around the words, his raspy voice yo-yoing up and down. Fascinated, her heart thumped as she listened. People passed by but nobody stopped, but she was enchanted, and so, feeling inside her pocket for a coin, she handed the pedlar her shiniest one. He regarded her tiny palm for a moment before throwing his head back on its wiry support, and squawking with laughter.

'Be off with ya, child,' he had said in a strange guttural accent, his mouth wide with blackened teeth, and Rosina had snatched her hand and dragged her away.

Ayda had craved books ever since.

A sound from outside drew Ayda back to the present. She left the barn and crept round to the back. There was a boy standing by an outside workstation. On it were several crates labelled in rapid handwriting and a pile of tools that definitely were not for the garden. Ayda looked on in amazement as two glass plates were removed from a contraption by the boy. The first was then fixed in a vice, sprinkled with some viscous mixture, the other quickly fixed above it.

Ayda crept closer to see more of what was going on; the boy's damp, black hair swaying in rhythm with the motion of his hands. A bird fluttered past aiming for the trees; a bee buzzed close to his head, but he didn't notice. Whatever he was doing had him too entranced to notice anything else, including her.

Eventually, he looked up and saw her.

'Hello! Would you like to see what I'm doing?' He smiled. 'It's all right, I won't bite, be nice to talk to someone, if truth be told…'

'What are you doing, sir?' Ayda asked.

'Look, just one thing first, could you not call me sir? Plain Adam will do fine.'

'I'm sorry … Adam.' She could feel her cheeks flush, and an embarrassed silence passed. 'I'm Ayda.'

'Well, Ayda. Can you keep a secret, I mean a real secret?'

'I love secrets,' she said, her feet fidgeting.

'I'm making an elliptical telescope, and it's a reflective one too.'

The words sounded fascinating and she repeated them, trying them out for size, knowing she wanted to hear more. But they didn't really explain much. What did an elliptical telescope do? She searched his face, but now he was busying himself with a greasy cloth.

'What's an elliptical telescope then?' The words fell out louder than intended.

Easing a bony hand through his hair, he walked over. 'To see the stars and the planets, Ayda. And here's another secret for you — one day, I'll build a machine to go into the sky so I can watch them from up there.' He pointed a finger at the blue above. 'Sit with them right up close, and no one will say it can't be done, because I *will* do it!'

They both looked up, savouring the dream for a moment before she glanced at his face: his jaw was set stubbornly, making him look older than his years, and very serious too. Perhaps he really meant it? As usual, questions crowded her mind, but could they really build things to fly in the sky? Walking to the empty tube, placing her hands on its rim, she peered down.

'Why are you grinding glass, Adam?' Somehow this mattered.

Taking a step back, he folded his arms. 'The glass plates are the telescope's mirrors. To achieve its correct reflective capabilities, it's crucial I grind them myself, then the light will reflect in the precise manner I want, and the images will be in sharp focus.'

Moving a boot slowly round, she looked up. 'The light from the stars gathers into your tube and is reflected by the mirrors up to our eyes. Is that right?'

'Almost, but a good try. The light is magnified through a lens in the eyepiece, and it's that image we see.'

'And the pink mixture, what's that for?'

'It's cerium oxide, a type of pink sand for polishing surfaces,' he said. 'Now, can I ask *you* something?'

She nodded.

'How are you both settling in? Your mother and yourself, that is er … Mrs de Corsi? Um, my mother considers her a first-class lady's maid.'

At this, Ayda looked away, then down at her scuffed boots, her toes brushing against their many holes, and her face grew warm with heat.

'Fine, thank you … Adam. Perfectly fine, but she will back soon, and I should be home.'

Adam coughed, clearing his throat. 'The mixture's a tad runny and I could do with some more powder. Would you mind fetching a bag from the barn, second drawer, third on the right, before you go?'

Ayda still wanted to know more about this mixture, so dipping her head she ran to the barn.

In no time, she was skipping through the entrance, smelling air stale with chalk, earth and mould. Before her stood a mahogany cabinet with well labelled drawers and after a cursory inspection, she located the second drawer and bag marked *Cerium Oxide grade FINE*. She lifted the bag, and quickly took it outside. The afternoon sun was already reflecting from the many windows of Dunthorpe House when she noticed a rounded figure bouncing down the steps.

'I've got to be going,' she said. 'Good luck with your telescope.'

'Did you see my books, Ayda?' he called after her. 'If you want, you may borrow them — any time.'

Ayda laughed with delight.

A week later, Ayda started her position as a pupil-teacher at the local elementary school. Her first impressions of St Theresa's were a disappointment. It was tiny, a single box-shaped room with floor-to-ceiling cupboards, rough floorboards, rotting windows and crumbling walls as cold as gravestones, where children from four to eleven would all be learning together.

Ayda shook herself, smoothing down her thick hessian skirt, trying to project confidence. She took a step forwards. A cacophony of children's chatter projected from the building, making her stomach lurch. Numbers *not* children had been her companions during childhood, as much a part of her as arms and legs, she could read them in her mind, conjure anything from them: calculations, formulae, equations, which she instinctively knew were right.

The day didn't begin well. With the old headmistress away, there was no one to meet her. The room's bare stone walls hemmed her in as she looked at the children: cross-legged, fidgeting, talking, unsettled, then at the rackety blackboard and thin chalk. No inspiration. No counting beads for little fingers. And no abacus. She would find one, she thought, feeling a lump in her throat. Opening cupboards, drawers, she stumbled into something unexpected — another room. She was not entirely sure she should be there, but straightaway she saw the abacus sitting on a desk smothered in papers.

The room was unusual. The walls were adorned with numbers and strange symbols. Dark bottles of every size sat above a cracked earthenware sink, images of the sun, moon and planets were plastered across the walls and light from the windows illuminated the liquids and peeling labels. Left of the sink, equations on a chalkboard spanned up and down, and on and on.

By now, Ayda was fascinated, inhaling the room's strange smells deep into her lungs: a mixture of mustiness and bad eggs. By the fireplace sat a desk at the foot of a mountain of books. Numbers were everywhere: on parchment and sheet paper. She instantly noticed the mistakes.

Frowning at the formulae, Ayda picked up a pencil, scribbling corrections in the margin. When she looked up again, she could hear voices chattering from the schoolroom. She stopped writing, and remembered the abacus.

'What are you doing in my private study, child?'

The voice belonged to someone she hadn't seen before: Mr Muir, the schoolmaster, a blanch-faced man with a large domed head and a thatch of red hair. Looking down, she saw his shoes shone in the dulled light, her own feet feeling heavy on the cold flagstones.

'You're Ayda de Corsi, the new pupil-teacher, aren't you?' He gently removed the sheet from her hand. 'I'm assuming your duties were made clear?'

'Yes, sir,' Ayda swallowed hard. 'I shouldn't have touched your things, only I was searching for the abacus. Someone must have taken it from the schoolroom, and then I saw the numbers and knew they were wrong.'

Mr Muir frowned and glanced down at the sheet. 'Sit down,' he said. 'Is this your own work?'

'Yes, sir.'

'And pray, who teaches you, child?'

'No one. I've always tried to go to school, but sometimes just read books instead.'

Mr Muir looked hard at her. 'Tell me, how do we find the area of a circle?'

'Pi multiplied by the square of the radius, sir.'

'And one of Newton's laws of motion?'

'Newton's second law states that force equals mass multiplied by acceleration.'

'Well, well, this is a turn for the better, eh? We'll have to see what can be done for you.'

Mr Muir arranged coaching for Ayda every fortnight, to teach her about mathematical logarithms, the elements, their properties, the earth, and the mechanics of life. The idea that the universe was limitless fascinated her — how did it start, where did it end, how deep was it?

But true to form, just as Ayda was starting to feel settled, her mother grew restless, and in December, they moved again, away from the Bound estate and nearer to St Theresa's in the village of Radlett. Rosina now took in washing, and from mutterings of a cruel *bastardo* at Dunthorpe House, Ayda gleaned some altercation had occurred there, but she was so relieved that her position at the school and her learning could continue, that she pried no further.

Although the loss of Adam's books pained her, the move turned out well, and by the following year, even her mother had settled, so that by the summer of 1913, Ayda's life revolved entirely around school, lessons and children. She had stability now, the stability she had always craved.

CHAPTER 2

Adam was sad to hear that Ayda had left the estate. He had been enchanted by her green eyes and curious nature. She had often borrowed his books, and he'd occasionally found her curled up in the barn, reading them. They had hardly spoken since that first day, though. She had been busy at the school and he was working hard on his experiments. He wished he hadn't been too shy to talk to her or at least say goodbye. And now it was too late.

Voices filtered down into the garden where Adam stood by the oak tree, and he looked up. Holed up in the upstairs library, Adam's father, Lord Bound, was finally getting the measure of his elder son.

'This is your home, you stupid boy, not a battlefield!' his father bellowed. 'I'll have no more mess, do you hear? Bloody pawprints all over their faces, and bodies. Downright clumsy, I say! Ram them by all means — we all did at your age, but no more slapping or kicking for pity's sake, understood?'

Granville's reply was inaudible, and Adam looked away disgusted, unsure his brother had even been punished. There had always been a swift turnover of servants at Dunthorpe House, but perhaps this would now change? Adam scratched his head, thinking. Beating a servant senseless could hardly be described as leaving *pawprints* like a muddied hound, but he wondered if his father understood this.

The library door slammed shut, and Granville emerged beneath the columned entrance: pale, twitching like an eel, and very unlike his usual brash self. An interview in Lord Bound's den meant a last chance — he would expect the matter resolved, and Adam hoped so too, for he hated unpleasantness.

Minutes later, his mother, Lady Clarissa, meandered down the Palladian steps in pursuit of her son, turning Adam's thoughts back to Ayda. Mrs de Corsi had left because of Granville, he was sure of it, and his mother had known what had gone on, but still had refused to speak up — why?

A crisp breeze whipped at Adam's hair as he crouched behind the tree, watching. Lady Clarissa was leaning heavily on Granville's shoulder, a bottle pressed to her side, her face as red as her auburn tresses as she petted and fawned over her favourite.

Angling himself to get a better view, he saw his mother stumble before being hauled up by Granville's free arm, and snorted in disgust. *What were they celebrating?* In any case, it didn't matter — he wasn't invited. Their laughter carried up through the branches as they ambled deeper into the verdure.

A rumbling in the distance made him wrench his gaze away, and spin round. A dark shape stuttered up the drive towards the house, glistening in the dying rays of daylight. The family's black Rolls-Royce Silver Ghost pulled up beside a black-browed Lord Bound who quickly boarded it, soon speeding away down the drive.

Adam swallowed the lump in his throat. He had tried to love this trio, he really had, but after eighteen years he'd had enough. A younger brother didn't matter here — his inventions and dreams only seemed to distance him more from the rest of his family.

It was getting late now, and Adam's thoughts turned to the advertisement sitting in his room:

WANTED

LARGE OUTBUILDING OR SHED

FOR PRIVATE COLLECTION OF FLYING MACHINES

Must be no more than 50 miles from London

Reply by return of post to:

Mr T. Shuttleby

Polworth House, Oxfordshire

His reply to Mr Shuttleby was in his hand and it was time it was posted, for this could be the start of a change in his fortunes. So, setting off down the winding drive past a terrace of stone cottages, in no time he had reached the red posting box at the far end of Aldenham village.

The sky was looking down on him watching, waiting, so he rewarded himself with an upward glance. Often, he had fantasised about chasing the white circles through the blue, sitting in the stratosphere or night sky, and since the first recorded flight in 1903 by the Wright brothers in America, he'd thought of little else.

Once you have tasted flight, you will forever walk the earth with your eyes turned skywards. How true those words were, but whereas da Vinci could only dream — *he* now had a chance! Instead of building flying machines, he would bring them home, offer them a sanctuary. The Bound estate was vast, desolate, secret, a perfect nesting ground for a flock of mechanical birds, the trio of lofty Old Sheds where his beloved telescope lay hidden, the perfect protection against prying eyes.

The letter in his hand fluttered through the posting box, and he felt his confidence soar. He might even impress his family — become a pilot — then they'd have to take note. He pictured himself looping the loop like France's Adolphe Pégoud or Russia's Petr Nesterov.

His dreams of building flying machines may have so far failed, but now things might just work out. He might even gain a friend too — God knows, he could do with one. He felt a strange affinity with the man he was writing to, like he knew him already. Surely that had to be a good omen? *When fears are grounded, dreams take flight.*

And perhaps Mr T. Shuttleby would make it all happen.

Things progressed rapidly. A friendship of sorts struck up between Adam and Thomas Shuttleby. They were of a similar age. Thomas was listed as both co-director in his family's furniture business, and as an aviator, owning five aircraft with his grandfather — until a fire had necessitated their removal.

Although Adam had provided the solution, he still felt unworldly and gauche by comparison, but there was no time to worry about that for transferring five flying machines hadn't been easy. Thomas had borrowed a car and a driver from his uncle who lived locally, and had then driven to Bicester, before flying each plane the fifty miles to Dunthorpe House. Once all the aircraft were installed, Thomas subjected each of the scrawny machines to a list of checks, and his own high standards.

'What a palaver,' Adam had said. 'Is all of this necessary?'

Thomas had smiled. 'I need to settle the flying machines into the area — see how the land lies, how much tree cover or clearance there is before I store them here. Important when flying, but what about you? Wouldn't you like a go, too?'

This had been music to Adam's ears. Luckily, no one seemed to notice the strange comings and goings at the far side of the estate, nor hear the hum of a propeller and thrum of an engine, even when the 1909 Blériot XI almost hit a tree. And by the time the last aircraft arrived, a 1912 Blackburn, Adam felt confident enough to check it himself — even fly it ten yards. With Thomas by his side, his confidence in the science of aeronautics had soared, though many people still considered those who flew show-offs and braggarts.

Adam was on his way to meet Thomas to attend a first meeting arranged by the local scientific community at Neptune Hall, in Elstree when he heard raised voices coming from the library. Things hadn't improved since Mrs de Corsi's departure: further resignations meant the new cook had left, the final straw being the footman's bloody nose. Adam lingered briefly outside the door, hearing his father's voice loud and clear.

'I'm sending you to Vancouver, in Canada, my boy,' Lord Bound was telling Granville, 'to your Uncle Rhys. In the outback you'll discover the difference between man and beast. Hard work there, I say, but it might just bring you round — make something of you. Your mother, of course, is inconsolable.'

'No, Father! You can't.'

Adam didn't hear his father's reply. He was pleased. His Uncle Rhys owned a large cattle farm in Vancouver and had something of a reputation for breaking in wild stallions. He wished him luck with Granville, but doubted even he could make a man from a beast. Checking the hallway clock, noting the time with a start, he made a bolt towards the Old Sheds — perhaps now *his* time would come?

A light breeze whistled through the Old Shed's broken shutters, oil glistening on the cobbled floor. The meeting today had been a close-call between flying lessons, but now, a black Model T Ford stood idling, waiting for him, spewing its cloudy mist over the nearest plane, its pasty-faced driver pushing oily fingers through his hair.

'Ready?' Thomas said as Adam appeared.

'I suppose so, though I can't understand why I'm talking about telescopes.'

Thomas changed gear, badly. 'We've been through this. And we agreed — aviation is too revolutionary. You have to trust me on this, Adam. I've attended scientific meetings before with my grandfather. Most are attended by crusty old men, and that's *his* opinion. Far better to speak of unlocking the stars. People are used to stars. One day someone will give a paper on aviation or aeronautics — maybe even you or me — just not today.'

Adam checked his wristwatch and balked. 'No one will be giving any paper if we don't get a move on.' Holding on to his cap, he felt the Model T lurch forwards to its maximum speed of forty miles per hour. Soon pastures and farmland were whirling past them, then at last, the modern square-blocked entrance of Neptune Hall came into view.

CHAPTER 3

Ayda had returned from the summer break to the news that Mr Muir had left the school.

'Mr Muir's role with St Theresa's has always come second to his research interests, my dear,' the headmistress had said, appraising Ayda from behind her desk. 'And we're so grateful for his help — when he can give it. Why, before you started, he was at Oxford for six months; indeed, that's why we employed you.'

Ayda smiled. 'It's no trouble at all, I can cope.'

Mrs Bellson's watery eyes smiled back. It was the right answer.

But within a few weeks, Mr Muir had returned, bounding into the schoolroom. Ayda was quietly reading *The Tale of Mrs Tittlemouse* by Beatrix Potter to her class, but at once they rose to their feet.

'I have so much to tell,' he had gasped, 'I hardly know where to begin. An invitation from the Royal Society, you see, I just got on a train and left…' He glanced guiltily at the children. 'But I see you've managed quite well, Ayda. Drop by my study at break time. Much to do now.'

At break, she had arrived at his study. It looked and smelled much as before, despite his absence; the desk was still piled with paper.

'Isn't it wonderful news? There's a local scientific gathering and I've been invited to give a paper. It's in two weeks' time. Naturally, Mrs Bellson was aware of the possibility.' He grinned at her. 'Did a stint back at home as well, in Linlithgow, then visited a friend, a Mr William Livens. Met him in '08 at

Christ's. Brilliant student and a crack shot with a pistol, I don't mind telling you.'

Ayda wondered how this was relevant but didn't interrupt.

'Of course, back then,' Mr Muir continued, 'I was a visiting lecturer, but we've kept up correspondence. Met again last month. Studied civil engineering, he did, he'll make his mark someday, I shouldn't wonder. Giving a paper here too — *Should science give us weapons for war?* So, what do you think, Ayda? Will you assist?'

Although thrilled to be asked, she hadn't been hugely impressed by Livens' subject matter: weapons for war sounded dreary. Still, it wouldn't do to disparage his friend. 'And where exactly are you giving this paper, sir?'

'Borehamwood way, so not too far from here. Place called Neptune Hall, just been built, I believe. Quite a ring to it, don't you think? Happened to meet the owners while I was away — real visionaries they are. Pioneers in the science of film making, would you believe? They plan to open as a studio early next year to make films, and they want people of science, people of standing to know their plans. All rather convenient, don't you agree?'

Ayda shrugged. 'I don't really know much about the science of film making, sir.'

Mr Muir frowned, and shook his head. 'I'm not sure you're getting my meaning, Ayda. You see, it's not just about film making. We've a wealth of scientific minds in the area and we're not that far from London either with our excellent rail links. We also have the advantage of clean air with none of that toxic pea-soup muck. Even the Royal Society have said they want to send one or two of their members just to see what we're about. Such an opportunity, Ayda — for the scientists of Hertfordshire. Such a modern building. too. It will put us on the map, make no mistake, and there's interest elsewhere: scientists from Birmingham University and two eminent German chemists holidaying in the area want to give papers as well. Mark my words, this will be the start of something big, who knows, maybe a future branch of the Society right here?'

Ayda listened on, thinking Mr Muir was getting ahead of himself as he twitched with excitement. Surely he knew the Royal Society had only ever been in London and didn't have branches? Perhaps it was time to bring him back down to earth, she thought, to steer him back to his favourite subject, himself. 'What paper have you decided on, sir?'

Mr Muir's shoulders sagged as he deflated like a balloon. 'God in heaven knows. That's the point. I can't decide. I was rather hoping you would.'

Mr Muir looked panicked, and unsettled by the challenges ahead. But what could be better than wading through all his research? The task was gargantuan, the timescale minuscule: years of experimentation plus all accompanying detritus in a mere two weeks … but what fun!

Now, Ayda was at Elstree station with Mr Muir, where he was fretting about his choice of paper. She was also fretting, but for a very different reason.

That morning, Ayda's mother had insisted Ayda wear her beautiful Italian silk blouse, and, while retrieving it from its paper-lined box, Ayda had chanced upon something shocking: a tattered old certificate. Her birth certificate. Rosina had always maintained that she had no information on Ayda's father. That he had abandoned her after she fell pregnant. But now she had discovered her father's name, and, after a loud and tearful harangue from Rosina, finally the facts of his life were squeezed out.

An Armenian Turk, his name was Adnan Gulzar. That she was no longer *de Corsi* was shocking. Adnan had travelled across the Strait of Otranto into Italy, and there he had stayed, falling in love with the country, its people … and with Rosina. Six months later, unrest had begun in Armenia with noises of a future militant uprising, and shortly after Ayda's birth, Adnan had left the arid rocky landscape of Pollenza, and returned to his homeland to 'sort some things out', but he had not returned. This signalled the start of Rosina's troubles, and her travels.

Brimming with so many questions, Ayda could barely speak. 'Mama, didn't you think I needed to know his name? When were you going to tell me about him?'

Looking guarded, Rosina shrugged her shoulders, offering no explanations other than it had happened so long ago. To her the matter was over and, as ever, when agitated, her command of English evaporated.

'He no write, so I forget him.'

Ayda tried in Italian but the subject was closed. A torrent of questions was unleashed in her mind — was her father tall, dark-haired like her? Did he laugh and smile a lot? Was his voice deep or soft — and were numbers his first language too? That she should find him there was no doubt, but soon her frustration turned on her mother. For sixteen years she had trusted Rosina, never questioned her judgement, only to be rewarded with this — so much for being a dutiful daughter! And the more she thought about it, the more she realised her mother's secrecy was selfish, her behaviour atrocious, but as she fumed, Rosina dug her heels in, refusing to talk.

This proved what Ayda had always known — that as mother and daughter, they were poles apart — not just in looks or intellect, but in everything. But did Rosina seriously think she would never think of him? And should she, as a nod to this man, now be known as Gulzar, *not* de Corsi?

The morning's events had made concentrating difficult. Mr Muir tutted at her lack of attentiveness as they approached Neptune Hall, where a heavy-jawed man in black guarded its impressive entrance. A trail of similarly dressed men could be seen snaking around the building, carrying papers in their portmanteaux: spectacled, grey-haired, most were older even than Mr Muir. Ayda joined the line, aware her heart was thumping, watching until at last, she could see the door.

When they were at the front of the queue, a thick arm came down upon her like a barrier, obstructing her entrance.

'I think you'll find everything's in order.' Mr Muir waved his invitation at the man in black, guarding the door. 'See here, Mr C. Muir *and* guest.'

'Sorry, guvnor,' the man said, wedging himself in front of Ayda. 'No ladies admitted to local scientific meetings.'

'But my invitation says…'

'Rules is rules, sir.' The man pointed a grubby finger. 'There's the Black Pot café 'cross the road, and The Crown yonder way, should the lady work up a thirst.'

Well, how dare he! Ayda's face burned as the complaining over the hold-up started behind her. A few greyheads jostled past her as if she was invisible, and, feeling too shocked for embarrassment, her body began to tremble. And after all that hard work!

'Here's tuppence for a cup of tea.' Mr Muir produced a coin, scurrying inside without looking back.

With the wooden doors now bolted, the hall hummed at her as she stood outside. Alone. The coin between her fingers fell to the ground. Her mouth was dry, her throat constricted. After a few minutes, sounds began emanating from inside the hall: chattering, coughs and splutters which somehow reached her and punctuated her solitude. Less than six feet from ground level, a shutter flapped above a stray pallet from The Crown, and she knew what she had to do. Climbing onto the pallet, she craned her neck forward, straining to hear through a small, leaded window, and forgot her outrage.

She could see — and hear — and that was all that mattered.

A young voice spoke, and Ayda started. She knew this voice, its soft calming tones. She raised her head towards it.

'*Reflectors versus refractors. When we see a reflection of a star in a highly polished piece of glass, can we really deduce that by simply rotating the glass to a different angle, we are unlocking the secrets of the universe? And if the light from the star were to bend, or refract…*'

Ayda listened, transported back to a hot summer's day over a year ago. Things had seemed simpler back then, though she felt for the owner of this voice now as she had then, hoping he was being taken seriously. Applause followed, then more voices. Someone announced the name William Howard Livens, Mr Muir's colleague. A silence descended as she stood on her tiptoes to get a clearer view.

'*Gentleman,*' a rich voice boomed. '*Should science give us weapons for destruction and war? I am but a humble civil engineer, perhaps not qualified to answer this, but a few months ago, I began experimentation on a weapon which I believe may be of immense, strategic importance.*' Livens cleared his throat. '*Where deployed, no man, animal, plant, nor stretch of land will be left untouched.*'

There were gasps. He paused again.

'*It will be deployed with the utmost stealth, buried in channels beneath the earth. It is but a simple construction, beautiful some would say, some fifty-six feet long using a long, tubular chamber rather like a telescope. This chamber, however, will contain fuel.*'

Louder gasps, and Ayda feared she would hear no more.

'Silence please, gentlemen. May I continue? Compressed gas will be pushed into the fuel chamber via pistons propelling the fuel, and finally a spark, a flame, ignition — the ultimate weapon, my friends, with the ultimate conclusion. And nothing in its path will survive the Livens Flame Projector...'

An icy chill spread through Ayda's bones; the murmuring in the Hall was now at fever pitch. A wobble started in her box, then she was over, sprawled on the ground just as two jovial voices rounded the corner laughing, clapping shoulders.

'What a meeting, and Moseley and Livens! Much better than some of the old windbags, though you can bet Livens will bang on about his fireworks for hours.'

'I agree, Thomas, but perhaps we should have stayed for questions?'

'Poppycock! Heard enough — quite scary really. Pint of beer what's needed. Hello, what's this?'

The two men stopped in front of her.

'Good grief ... it's... Is it you, Ayda?'

She looked up from the ground. The voice belonged to a tall young man with black hair flopping over a familiar face, his pitch-black eyes fixed upon her.

'Yes. Hello, Adam, I heard you earlier. Very well done!'

He smiled as he helped her to her feet. 'Um, how is your mother, Mrs de Corsi?'

Ayda grimaced and didn't reply.

'Mother still misses her,' Adam continued, his eyes flashing. 'Granville has attacked more servants since she left — but no more. Father's sending him to Canada, and good riddance, I say!'

Ayda took a step back. 'I'm afraid I didn't realise,' she said, recalling something Rosina had said. 'But my mother, I'm sure, will be most interested in this news.'

Thomas cleared his throat, pointedly. 'The Crown? We'd better get in before the crowds. Will you join us, Ayda?'

Over a drink, Ayda talked of St Theresa's, and memories of her time at Dunthorpe House. 'How is your reflecting telescope, and all those wonderful books?' she asked Adam.

'They're all fine, Ayda … and missing you terribly.' Adam looked away.

Thomas and Adam continued discussing their flying machines, and her green eyes widened at the descriptions. Mr Muir's lessons had helped open her eyes to the possibility of flight, but what they were working on still seemed unbelievable. The thought of flying in one of these machines made her feel lightheaded — almost giddy. *Well, why not*, she thought, intending to broach the subject. Then she heard another voice.

'For goodness' sake, there you are! I've been searching all over,' Mr Muir said gruffly. 'We'll be running along now; Ayda, I haven't got all day. I've several copies of my papers to distribute — that's assuming you brought the extras? There's much interest here and I shouldn't wonder if I make my mark today.' He gave a cough. 'Come along now. Please!'

Sensing her embarrassment, Adam stepped in. 'Emmeline Pankhurst is to make a speech in the next village. I say, you don't fancy hearing her afterwards, do you? We could make a foursome with your friend, here?'

Mr Muir looked affronted but Ayda would dearly like to hear Mrs Pankhurst's speech. She knew the Suffragette movement had been gaining momentum, and her exclusion from the meeting today had really struck a nerve. She looked again at Mr Muir's red face and her heart sank.

'Some other time perhaps?' she said to Adam.

Returning home after the meeting, Ayda found Rosina anxiously pacing their tiny cottage.

Despite their argument that morning regarding her father, Ayda's heart went out to her. 'Mama, why didn't you tell me what happened at Dunthorpe House — that you'd been hit?'

Rosina folded her arms. '*Non importante*!'

Ayda held her arms out to her mother in despair, wondering what else she was hiding. 'Of course it is important, but he's gone now. For good. Banished to Canada.'

'*Chi*?'

'Granville, Mama.'

Propelling herself upright, Rosina grabbed her shawl and fastened on her shoes.

'Where are you going?' Ayda asked.

'I go back. Back to *bella signora*, I go back to work for Clarissa.'

'But what about *my* work? Remember, I work at the school. Here.'

Pursing her lips, Rosina said, 'We go back. You can walk from there.'

Ayda had seen that look before and knew there was no point arguing.

When Rosina returned later that evening, it was to tell Ayda that she had been given back her old job with its accommodation.

'*Ecco cara*, we move again, *questa `e la fine*.'

Ayda shrugged her shoulders. Yes, her own work would be further away, but maybe her mother might be happy at long last. And then she was smiling. Adam, his books, *and* the flying machines would be there too. And why shouldn't *she* learn about these wonderful mechanical birds now they were captive on the estate? Could this move finally be a step in the right direction?

CHAPTER 4

Ayda and her mother had returned to the cottage on the Bound estate and a few weeks after seeing Ayda in Elstree, Adam wrote her a note: *I am sure you would like a respite from the rain and if you still love secrets, please meet with like-minded people at the Old Sheds, tomorrow, 3 p.m. A.B.*

He didn't expect a reply but he hoped to see her there. After he had returned from delivering it, Adam headed towards Dunthorpe House's Banqueting Hall with its Jacobean gilded ceilings and ornate plasterwork, then stopped. From outside the door, Adam could hear his father's voice already percolating out into the corridors. He sighed, knowing that since Granville had been packed off to Canada, it fell to him to listen to his father's political pontifications over breakfast even though they inhabited different worlds with neither understanding the other's.

'I've been charged with keeping an eye on two veterans from the Boer. What d'you think of that, boy?' Lord Bound demanded as Adam entered the room.

Seating himself as far away from his father as the mahogany table would allow, Adam cast a longing look at the window.

'I've too many responsibilities, and it saddens me that my family show me no interest or concern,' Lord Bound snapped.

Adam stared in disbelief. He'd survived his whole life without interest or concern from his father, but mentioning this now wouldn't be wise. Then a shadow darkened the doorway. Adam looked up to see his mother standing there, dressed to the gunnels in sapphire silk, a stole of sable softly draped across her shoulders. Lady Clarissa cleared her throat, eyeing the sherry decanter at the far end of the room.

'I've been invited for cocktails at two,' she began brightly, slipping into a chair. 'Which of you two will accompany me?' Her question sat as flat as the table before her.

Outside, thick cumulus clouds were darkening the sky with any hopes of flying fading fast before Adam's eyes. Now focussed on his newspaper, Lord Bound sipped his coffee, ignoring his wife to glance briefly in Adam's direction.

Adam regarded his mother. When had they last spoken?

'Gervaise,' she turned to her husband. 'I should like to attend Mim's cocktail party. Will you accompany me?'

Lord Bound shifted his newspaper. A fist landed on the mahogany table making Adam jump, a kedgeree dish crashing to the floor. 'Is that all you can bloody well think about? Don't you realise we've bred a pair of misfits?'

'Stop it, Gervaise,' his wife hissed, 'before you say something you will regret.'

'*Je ne regrette rien*, my dear — our eldest is only fit to inhabit the wilds of Canada — our youngest,' he paused to jerk a hand at Adam, 'has his head quite literally in the clouds these days. You, young man,' Lord Bound's eyes whipped to Adam, 'need to get a hold on the mess this country's in. Let me see now. There's a blue-blooded lunatic on the rampage abroad, by Jove, who's already got rid of Bismarck and his three successors. And dear old Wilhelm, he'll be causing trouble sooner or later, mark my words — another one too big for his boots! Thinks we should kowtow to him because of his blue blood.'

'But isn't his mother Queen Victoria's firstborn?' Adam said.

'What difference does that make, boy? His uncle is *King*. And now, everyone's panicking, and I've been told to think about a war cabinet — just like that!' He snapped his fingers. 'None of them capable of making a decision if their life depended on it — and who knows — perhaps it might?'

Lady Clarissa gripped the edge of the table. 'A cabinet of war? What are you talking about, Gervaise? Trying to scare me again, overdramatic as always. Have a care!'

A sparkle in the windowpane made Adam sit up, a glow of orange in the distance lit up the field like a tinder box, and then the room fell into darkness. Baxter, the butler, appeared.

'It's the generator, sir,' he announced.

'Well, see to it, please,' Lord Bound barked, 'and bring the car round. I'll drive myself to town, the line might be flooded.'

'Is that wise, dear?' his wife enquired. 'What of the roads?'

But with his mind made up and in no mood for further conversation, Lord Bound departed to his chambers, leaving Lady Clarissa to summon her lady's maid for support.

Adam glanced at Mrs de Corsi steering his mother away, struck by the contrast: one rounded, the other paper-thin, one caring, the other indifferent, and he thought briefly of Ayda, how lucky she was. But his father's talk had affected him too — a war cabinet meant discussions on weapons, machinery, equipment — maybe even a future for people like him. Aeroplanes were the ultimate form of transport, the eyes of the future, not just a bird's eye view of the world: they could transport people and supplies long distances, even across the Channel, he knew, remembering Monsieur Blériot.

There *had* to be a role for him somewhere — but first he would need to obtain his Aero Club Aviator's Certificate, or 'ticket' as it was widely known. And so, he joined his father in the black Rolls-Royce as it set off towards London: he was headed for Hendon Aerodrome.

A lot had changed at Hendon since Adam had last visited, and now he was a pilot too, well, almost, he thought, making his way towards a flattened area of green by the Hall Flying School where another group of would-be aviators had assembled. Most were from the military whilst others, like Adam, were private pilots. They were all gathered round an old single-engine biplane.

To Adam's critical gaze, the school's machine, nicknamed the 'cauldron', looked cumbersome and slightly bizarre with its stubby nacelle, single tractor engine, equipment and fuel stores aligned in a slab-like arrangement. At the back, the twin-boomed tail was exposed, the rudders, like shark fins, were fronted by spruce and ash wings and a wooden two-blade propeller, all making it look unusual and rather ugly.

He stood with the others, eyeing the thick cloud cover, waiting for the weather to improve, until at midday, like a curtain opening, the sky suddenly lit up with sunshine. On the green, the smell of cut grass and wet earth made Adam's nostrils twitch while he waited his turn, his legs shaking with nerves and longing.

'Next.'

Finally, he was up. Climbing into the front seat, Adam felt like he had sunk into a bathtub. Glancing around the cockpit, there wasn't much there: elevator stick, rudder bar but no throttle, and no engine switch. He shook his head trying to remember something Thomas had said: *Some planes are very simple and all about weight. No throttle means less weight, so engine on-off becomes the only way of controlling speed.* And feeling down the side, there it was. An engine switch. He let out a breath, his confidence flooding back. He knew the theory, but now it had to be put into practice. Then he noticed the wires ... lots of them. Not unexpected really because like the Blériot, the plane's roll was controlled by warping wires. Inspection over, he felt better, his legs no longer shaking, and the examiner was walking his way.

'Right then, sir. Know the drill, do you?'

The thin man was flipping the pages of a clipboard by the lower wing.

'I do indeed, sir.'

Eyes still on his board, the examiner sighed. 'Right then. I want no funny business, do you hear? We've got four more after you today, so just get her up to two hundred feet, get her round the circuit, do your figures of eight then down again nice and slow, then engine off — if you please.'

'Certainly, sir,' Adam said, priming the carburettors, so desperate was he to get in the air. But the examiner talked on.

'See that post over there by the school? The one that's all scratched and bent? That's where you stop, okay, not on it but by it. And remember, no high jinks.' Before Adam could reassure him, the man had moved to the propeller where a mechanic stood waiting.

Fuel on, *engine on*, then Adam leant over the side.

'Contact,' he shouted.

The mechanic got the two-blade propeller turning and the Anzani engine sprang to life. With the familiar smell of oil in his nostrils Adam took a deep breath. He needed this. Needed this ticket more than anything.

'Right then,' he said to himself, fiddling with the stick. The plane began moving fast, a little too fast, and flicking the engine off, he adjusted it ready for take-off. Soon he was bumping along the grass, the nose lifting as he eased the stick back, the wheels leaving the grass — yes, he'd done it — got the feel of the plane. And there it was again. That unmistakeable euphoria that flight always gave him, his mood lifting in tandem. The little plane continued its ascent and was soon skimming the tops of a group of trees at the far end, then see-sawing a bit before flattening out at around two hundred feet. A blue blanket of sky spread out before him; he wanted to go higher but recalled the examiner's instructions.

Looking over the side, a shrunk-down Hendon was moving in slow motion. Planes were taxiing in and out of hangars, taking off, landing, being re-fuelled or taken apart and fixed. The hum of the rotary engine and the whoosh of the wind in the warping wires calmed him, and he looked over again, amazed at the view. The clouds were still behaving, and the visibility afforded by a smaller lower wing was spectacular. And then the wind picked up and the plane started yawing.

'Concentrate!'

Foot to the rudder bar, the nose pulled up slightly and he remembered Thomas's warning: *Don't use the yaw at slow speeds else it might stall.* A quick calculation showed he was averaging fifty miles per hour — just enough. Down below, the mangled post poked up at him, and Adam changed direction having completed his first circuit.

Two distance flights of at least three miles and one hundred and eighty-five yards in length. Around seven miles southeast lay the city of London, but twenty miles northwest was home. And with a full tank, how easy would it be to head back there and surprise everyone, make them look up at him — even his parents? Another burst of wind wobbled the plane, restoring his focus, and he remembered the task in hand. Completing his first figure of eight, he changed direction. Ten minutes later, he had completed a series, his manoeuvres now all done. With a heavy heart he switched off again, reducing speed, ready for his descent: one hundred and fifty feet, one hundred feet, his skin warming, fifty feet, a figure just visible by the post. Down he went, holding the plane steady, bouncing only twice on the grass, flicking the engine on then off, taxiing fifty yards to the post, before switching off for good. He was unfastening his helmet when someone leant into the cockpit.

'Pass!' the examiner bellowed, still holding his clipboard. 'Next.'

Adam jumped down smiling, seeing the next would-be pilot approach.

'Good luck, old boy,' he said, patting his shoulder. And as he left the field, the words *no funny business*, followed him out. Ahead, Hendon was as busy as ever with a plume of smoke funnelling upwards, a fire-engine clattering towards the third runway to someone not as fortunate as him. But even that didn't dampen Adam's spirits.

Two hours later, only two tickets had been issued, with a full twelve candidates of army personnel failing: Adam's number 658 was one of the two. Wheeling the biplane away, a small, grubby-faced mechanic shook his head and took a swig from a flask.

'Problem, sir?' Adam enquired politely.

'You bet. Don't know whether I'm coming or going.' An oily cloth passed liberally over the man's brow. 'Look at them warping wires and tail boom, and the truss. All need fixing — again! Like this every day for the past month. They comes along: lieutenant this, captain that, private la di dah, sometimes twenty in a day. Never seen a bus before, but still they comes. Not a clue! Most crash, then they expect me to have it as right as rain by the morrow when it all starts again.'

The melancholy mechanic scowled, taking a longer swig from his flask and just then 'Bound 658' sounded across the airfield.

'That's me.'

Royal Aero Club Ticket 658 was issued to the Honourable Adam Bound and Adam stared at it with pride. Something good had finally happened: a recognisable qualification stipulating he had sufficient control of an aircraft to participate in all the Club's contests and displays.

A pilot at last, he thought, and there were two people he couldn't wait to tell…

CHAPTER 5

Just before 2 p.m. the following day, wrapped in two woollen shawls, Ayda set off from St Theresa's, wearing her only pair of boots. The last time she had spoken to Adam, they had talked only briefly of flying machines, but today she hoped she would see one in real life.

But half a mile into her walk, sheets of icy rain lashed down. With each step, her skirt dragged through muddy puddles, soaking up the water like a sponge. She turned back, wishing she had heeded her doubts, but minutes later, a parping noise stopped her in her soggy tracks. A black Model T Ford had stopped at the roadside, its door flung open. Instantly, she recognised Adam as the goggle-faced driver in a thick overcoat.

'Get in.'

Such was the rain's ferocity, Ayda complied without question and soon, through the steady slosh of the wiper blade, a trio of white sheds blurred into view.

'What in God's name possessed you to walk?'

A puddle had developed on the floor as she unwrapped her layers. 'I wasn't thinking properly.'

'Clearly. Well, if you'd let me know, I'd have sent the car round. Anyway, we're here now.'

She watched as Adam parked the Model T, aware that her clothes were still soaking.

'Borrow these,' he said, and a dirty pair of overalls was thrust at her. 'You can change behind that oil can. No one will see.'

Just as he said this, Thomas emerged from behind the life-sized drum, and walked over. Bluish-white smoke billowed out from the recesses behind him, and looking around, Ayda saw that everything was coated in grease.

'Let me introduce you to the machines,' Adam said, propelling her past Thomas. 'It's why I invited you here in the first place — Thomas's collection is now accommodated here, all the way from Bicester.'

'But Oxfordshire's miles away, couldn't anything be found closer?'

'Not really. Anyway, it's a perfect location, secluded, ideal for research.'

'Research?'

'We're hoping to build our own machine.' Adam pointed to an area of more bluish-white fumes.

Five mosquito-like structures stood amidst the decay. Ayda's jaw dropped open.

'Let me show you.' Adam guided her over to them. 'That's a 1909 Blériot Mark XI.' The first contraption had a distinctive metal rod onto which a network of wires converged. Ayda recognised the now famous plane from newspaper pictures.

'Oh yes, Louis Blériot and the first Channel flight.'

'That's right. And that's a 1910 Bristol Boxkite. Then there's the 1910 Deperdussin.' Adam pointed at a particularly scrawny specimen. 'And over here, we have a 1911 Avro Triplane, and finally our most modern machine — a 1912 Blackburn monoplane.'

Ayda examined it: half exposed, rain splashing down on its canvas, tiny droplets hanging from its wires like pearls on a necklace, spray bouncing onto the wooden surfaces below. Pulling a face, she dodged beneath the wing. 'It looks a bit neglected, Adam.'

'Oh, it's not neglected, I can assure you, but it'd be happier up there.' He pointed up at the steel-grey sky. 'So, Ayda, would you like to fly it?'

On the following Wednesday, the sun shone as Ayda arrived at the Old Sheds. Burdened with doubts, she wasn't quite sure why she had come: curiosity and something in her head telling her to. As she walked from the school, her emotions had leapt from elation to fear, making her stop at least once to take stock. And now she was here.

She approached the trio of sheds. Adam and Thomas were chatting by the Blériot, Adam's arm flung casually over its wing. They didn't look nervous, so why was she?

'Ah, there you are!' Thomas said. 'Thought you'd changed your mind.'

Beside him, Adam shook his head. 'Nonsense, Thomas. Wasn't I just saying how Ayda is different from other people?'

But Ayda wasn't listening, her attention focussed on a strange contraption, its frame more skeletal than she remembered, its wiry wings flexing like an angry insect in the breeze. Her face blanched. Was this what she was going to fly? Could it accommodate one person let alone two?

'Right then, let's get started,' Adam said. 'The oil drum's just round the corner, remember? Here's your overall, boots, and flying jacket.' Adam flung miscellaneous items at her, Ayda almost dropping the thickest, heaviest jacket she had ever held.

'Do I need to wear all this? I've brought some extra shawls, and —'

'Look, Ayda, I'll be surprised if we clear fifty feet today, but I can tell you, you will feel cold. Now, put the clothes on — please.'

Five minutes later, Ayda was dressed in the heavy clothes, mufflers and helmet, the clunky boots making it hard to walk. Adam was already scrunched inside the Blériot, and Thomas was stationed by the propeller.

'I've got just under an hour, so let's get going,' Adam said, beckoning her over. 'Right then. Look around — see all the steel wires? They're warping wires. They allow the wings to warp or twist to control the roll of the plane.' Ayda looked around the cockpit, there were indeed wires everywhere, but Adam was still talking. 'Now press down here on the rudder bar, see how the tail moves? This will control the yaw of the plane — do you know what yaw is?'

She nodded, seeing the tail of the Blériot move up then down. 'It's the rotation about a vertical axis,' she told him, 'and roll is rotation nose to tail, and pitch is the movement around a side to side axis.'

Adam's eyebrows shot up. 'Very good. Well, if that's all clear, we may as well get moving. But first, the engine needs to be primed with fuel. Then we can start off, and it's full throttle and full stick forward to get power here because the tail can be a bit heavy.'

As Ayda primed the engine, the cockpit flooded with fumes, and she wrinkled her nose.

'Now shout "Contact" to Thomas and he'll get the prop going which will draw more fuel into the cylinders.'

'The prop?'

Adam pointed. 'That's the propeller, Ayda, where Thomas is waiting. And when we're moving, I mean *really* moving, and you'll know when, we'll pull back on the stick nice and easy, and off she goes.'

Inside her mufflers and helmet, Ayda smiled to herself, liking the idea that the Blériot was female.

'Oh, by the way, I forgot to mention that the castor oil and fuel might make you nauseous, and of course, there's the bouncing up and down, so if it's all too much, I'll get you down.'

Ayda shook her head. 'I'll be fine.'

'Good. Well, go on, then — Thomas is waiting.'

'Oh, I see. Okay, then. Contact!'

The little plane sprung to life, spitting and coughing, every morsel of its construction juddering. Ayda too felt like she had just awoken and her body started to tingle. With her hand on the control stick, they started moving faster. Moving it further forward made the plane go even faster, the noise becoming deafening. And then Adam was waving his hands about, tapping the control stick. It was time.

Hands together, they eased the stick back, and like magic, the nose lifted, the wheels leaving the ground, everything below starting to shrink. She was flying. Up and up they climbed, the wind rushing over her like she wasn't there, chilling her despite her layers.

They kept climbing for what seemed like ages but was in fact only a few minutes, and Ayda looked around her. Above, the clouds were larger than she had ever seen, but everything below — the sheds, Thomas — was much smaller. The control stick moved again, and Ayda was aware the pitch was changing, that they were banking into a turn. After another circuit of the sheds they banked again, this time turning in the other direction.

Adam was watching. He removed his hand and foot, while Ayda kept her foot on the rudder bar, doing the movements herself. Inside she was smiling, feeling the Blériot's heartbeat through the stick, loving the view … and the freedom.

And then she was throttling back, losing height, almost gliding, the ground fast approaching, everything large again, the wheels skipping, bouncing along like a ball. Then there was an almighty thud and it was done.

Adam shot her a look, asking if she was feeling all right.

She grabbed his hand. 'Oh, that was brilliant, Adam. So much fun — when can we do it again? What about next Wednesday?'

He looked at her weakly. 'Who knows, Ayda? Always look for clues in the sky. Watch it. Learn to read it — like a book.'

Ayda nodded. She liked that. 'Like a book,' she muttered.

CHAPTER 6

For the next month, the weather had other ideas. Rain and high winds each day made flying impossible. On the first clear Wednesday five weeks later, a black Model T Ford drew up outside St Theresa's Elementary School. Wrapped in an assortment of shawls, Ayda slipped out just after lunch, hoping nobody would notice. But Cameron Muir was circling the car, his dome-shaped forehead creased into a frown.

'What's all this about, Ayda?'

'I have an appointment, sir, and…' She paused. 'Wednesday is my half-day.'

'Why of course it is,' Mr Muir said, still looking at the car. 'But make sure you're here promptly tomorrow, I fear there will be much to do.'

Ayda nodded, getting into the car, smiling at Adam.

The lesson started as soon as she was dressed, Adam allowing her to prime the engine and check the rudder and warp wires. She was about to shout "Contact" when he stopped her.

'We need to talk about wind direction and lift, Ayda.'

Inclining her head, she smiled. 'I know all about that, and I've already noted its direction; it's a north-westerly, so if we are to achieve greater lift, we must take off into it. And land into it too.'

Adam stared at her. 'Well, if that's all straight with you, Thomas is waiting — and another thing, it's been over a month, do you remember the controls?'

By now, she was desperate to get airborne. 'I do, Adam, I remember it all. Contact!'

She had given the order. At full throttle the Blériot started moving, gaining speed, Ayda waiting for that irresistible moment: that kick in the back, that flutter in the pit of her stomach telling her it was time. Time to fly. Up and up, the little plane rose, one hundred feet, then settling at just over two hundred feet. Adam kept his hands away from the control stick, and Ayda felt the same trembling of excitement, of freedom as before. Up here there was nothing to judge her except a clear blue sky and the laws of physics, the world above much fairer than the one below. Looking over the side, the ground seemed more distant today, the Old Sheds less defined, less bright. The Bound estate stretched out in every direction like a green carpet: areas with trees or small forests, an orchard or an area strewn with rocks and crags, and rolling fields. All had boundaries. But there were no boundaries in the sky.

Like before, Ayda banked and turned using both rudder and control stick, fine-tuning her movements so the plane could twist and turn. Adam sat back, enjoying the view and the ride, only once taking control when he thought the engine might stall. Passing her a note, he asked her to calculate the speed, and after a few seconds, she wrote forty-five mph, to which he nodded. But would he allow her to land? While debating this, she had already throttled down, the plane slowing and drifting into the wind. And by the time he had decided she was probably ready, they were bouncing along the grass and coming to a rest. She had done it already.

'My goodness, you learn quickly. Have you been stealing my Blériot during your breaktime and practising in secret?'

'If I only I could,' said Ayda, removing her goggles. 'But when something interests me, I learn fast. And I've had five weeks to think about it.' She looked around to see Thomas approaching.

'Ah, there you two are!'

Adam quickly moved to join him, leaving Ayda alone by the Blériot with her thoughts: how easy it would be to jump back in and fire it up again. As if reading her mind, Adam was suddenly by her side, his voice now a whisper. 'Keep reading that sky and I'll see you next time.'

The weather worsened, drowning the village and the Bound estate. Sandbags were rolled out, people eyeing the nearby rivers as gales and rain ravaged the county. Ayda watched the sky for the next two months praying for a break. When there was one and a dark shadow pulled up outside the school, she couldn't contain her delight. At least, Adam and she were on the same page. Ready with shawls wound round her shoulders, she had left by the time Mr Muir noticed the black Model T on the main street.

Ayda changed extra quickly behind the oil drum, while Adam squeezed himself into the Blériot.

'I had thought this would be your last lesson before going solo, but you might find you've forgotten a few things, and...' He saw Ayda's head was shaking.

'How can you be so sure?'

She shrugged. 'Can't we just see. If you correct anything, anything at all — then I'm not ready.'

'Agreed.'

This time, the plane rose higher and higher, Ayda's fingers tingling from cold, her spine shivering in the thinner, cooler air. The world opened out before her with the promise of more: wider and more beautiful. The Blériot hummed away to itself as if glad to be out at play, and she wondered which direction should she go in? She looked at Adam, but his arms were folded, his head drooping slightly. Perhaps he was asleep? Her decision then. To the northwest, the River Beane was in spate, shimmering a silvery blue. Directly west, the tall square belfry of St Albans medieval Clock Tower was an excellent landmark. Where should she go? Ayda felt for the compass in her jacket, conscious of an odd vibration in the plane's tail. Perhaps she should fly the same distance as Louis Blériot did four years before. Around twenty miles, she thought, moving rudder and control stick so the plane circled. What about going to London? She'd always fancied visiting the capital. And the King.

The plane wobbled. The wind had suddenly picked up, the howl in the warping wires sounding above a noiseless engine. The vibrations had also stopped too, no spluttering, no thudding noise. Beside her, Adam stirred. That settled it — they wouldn't be going to London. In her head, she recalled something Thomas, the voice of experience, had said: *Learn to glide. These planes are perfect gliders. It might just save your life — engines are like humans, they sometimes rest.*

She hoped Thomas was right. Adam's hand moved over the control stick, but she shook her head, and moved it away. She knew how to glide. The plane whistled on for a mile or so, the trio of white sheds visible. Adam was pointing now. A group of trees lay beyond the grassy area of the first shed. The plane drifted lower and lower. At about one hundred feet from the ground, the engine spluttered back to life and the nose rose, the thumping from the propeller drowning out the wind. *Thank God.* Swooping down in a smaller circuit, Ayda gently throttled back, willing the engine not to stall again, the green grass looming closer, the earth dashing up to greet them.

Thomas came to meet them. 'I say, that was an excellent landing, but it looked like you were gliding earlier.'

'We were. Let's just say it was an interesting journey.' Ayda's legs were shaking as she climbed down. 'Very interesting indeed.'

A lump was in her throat — and for once, she felt proud recalling where she had been, and what she had done.

'Engine stalled again, surely not?'

Adam nodded, then glanced at Ayda.

'Yes, well, she handled it really well — you or I couldn't have done any better. So as far as I'm concerned, she's ready.'

'Ready?' asked Ayda.

'Yes. Next time you can go solo. Today showed you didn't really need me. But there'll be more lessons too: the Bristol. Then the Blackburn…'

Ayda swallowed hard. Solo? It sounded so final. Was she really ready? Adam *had* been with her today — there if she needed him. And only time would tell if she did.

CHAPTER 7

Two months later, Ayda embarked on her first solo flight.

Checking wind direction, crosswinds, taxiing straight, bumping here and there, Ayda pursed her lips.

Take-off requires full forward on the elevator stick to counteract any tail heaviness. Adam's voice was clear in her head. *The tail has to be lifted very high in this machine to get any acceleration, and when it appears to be going as fast as it can, then pull back a little on the stick pressure, and it will lift off nicely.*

He was right. As before, pushing the stick forward made the plane go faster. It was easy! The three white sheds sped past in a misty blur, the green of the grass, the brown of the thicket fading fast, the wind rattling across everything, the little plane screaming as the wind whipped around its piano wires. It was time. Gently easing back on the stick, the nose lifted as if by magic, and the Blériot XI climbed in a near perfect take-off. Ayda was bursting with pride.

Within seconds, the sky spread out in front of her, the world in miniature looking so beautiful from above that she knew it would be easy to just sit back, admire the vast expanse and forget about what she was doing. Climbing to three hundred feet, again the sheer force and power both alarmed and excited her, the wind buffeting the Blériot's wings, tailplane and fin, making its warping wires whine, which ensured her concentration didn't waiver for long. Experimenting with the rudder, she found she could still roll, bank, steer and keep steady, so, dipping her wing, she performed two perfect circuits of the sheds' perimeter. Moving up, then down, as if she were riding a giant flying see-saw, made her giddy with emotion.

The wind chilled her to the bone, and the stench of oil thrown out sickened her to the pit of her stomach, but still she smiled. She couldn't help it … she'd never had so much fun. Glancing over the side, two tiny figures were waving frantically below, but the engine's hum reassured her. Adam had said to feel it, to feel how the plane was sitting. She asked the Blériot how it was sitting, feeling the plane hum its reply that it was as happy as she was. *I have survived, I am flying by myself, and I love it better than anything else!*

After two more circuits, she came to a decision. This was what she wanted to do. She wanted to fly.

Flying somehow felt very solid, very safe, and she would show all those grey-haired men in Hertfordshire — indeed any man who thought she wasn't worthy — just how worthy she was. A quick glance at the oil pressure gauge made her plan her descent. Again, Adam's words rang in her ears: *Push the stick forward slightly for a slow descent, and always fly it to the ground with a level altitude. Stay like that till you can no longer hold the tail up, then let it fall and pin it with your stick back.*

She flew on, reducing the throttle slowly, easing the tail down, managing a near perfect landing, before taxiing up to a beaming Adam. Thomas was wheeling out the 1910 Bristol Boxkite biplane, winking at her as she approached. Feeling her colour rise, she smiled back at him as he mouthed 'well done' before turning back to the Boxkite.

Days later, winter finally yielded to spring, and then summer, and a pattern was established of Wednesday-afternoon flying at the Old Sheds. While Adam and Thomas designed their own aircraft, Ayda also helped service the planes now she was an integral part of the workforce.

The following Wednesday, Ayda arrived early for her lesson. Soon, deep in discussion with Thomas, she rubbed her oily hands down her overalls and started measuring with a long tape. Then, grasping the diagram and plans from Thomas's hand, she scribbled some numbers, before smiling, satisfied.

'That's it,' she said. 'That will work perfectly. Lift-off and a good thrust will be achieved with minimum drag. See?'

Adam hung back, consulting his wristwatch, until Thomas called him over, grinning with delight a while later.

'I think we've got the wing-to-wing ratio sorted.'

'Oh, well done, that's a weight off my mind,' Adam grasped his hand. 'How the dickens did you do it?'

Thomas shifted his gaze. 'Well, as much I'd like to take the credit, it should all go to Ayda.' Not looking up, she continued on with her work. 'Our resident mathematician here just glimpsed at the drawings, measured a few things and said to use the Golden Ratio — Fibonacci's ratio. You know, the one that's everywhere: in nature, in flower petals, seashells, everything. Make the ratio of the two wingspans 1.61803, she said. And you'll never guess what? It all fits perfectly — like God designed the wings himself.'

Adam nodded.

Later, Ayda trudged back through sunny cornfields. She'd left the Old Sheds early feeling disappointed, but couldn't fathom out why. Perhaps she hadn't flown for long enough? Today she hadn't spent much time with Adam, and wondered why this mattered.

Over the last few months, Adam had become a true friend: his encouragement and unwavering belief in her abilities really helped her confidence, though his friendship wasn't the only reason she walked to the sheds every week. She wanted to better herself, achieve something she was capable of — but today she had felt small … and troubled. She couldn't help thinking on the current political situation. Thomas had told her earlier that the situation abroad had improved — that David Lloyd George, the Chancellor of the Exchequer, had stated that the mood was good, that relations with Germany were infinitely friendlier than they had been for years.

'What did I tell you, Ayda? All that scaremongering after Christmas was a load of poppycock! They'd never let on if there was going to be any trouble.'

'Thomas,' she had said, 'what if Mr Lloyd George was doing exactly what you've just said, not letting on that there *is* going to be trouble. What if what he said was in fact a lie?'

'Have a little faith, Ayda, please. A member of Asquith's government wouldn't lie to the nation, and not on New Year's Day either. There's a lot you don't understand, nor are you supposed to.'

Despite her abilities, her opinion had been dismissed — she was a woman, and valued much like a child. With her head aching and her feet tingling — a sure sign from old that something was wrong — she felt convinced something bad would happen. But what, and when?

CHAPTER 8

On the 30th June, 1914, Sir Arthur Nicolson, a British Ambassador in St Petersburg, reported in the *Times*: *The tragedy which has just taken place in Sarajevo will not, I trust, lead to further complications.*

Two day before, Archduke Franz Ferdinand of Austria and his wife Sophie had been assassinated. Rumours abounded everywhere. At St Theresa's, the children looked anxious, subdued, the older ones broaching questions that had gone unanswered at home.

Ayda's head ached, and her toes tingled as she faced the classroom.

'Miss, is there going to be a war?'

'I have no idea, Billy. Please finish your sums.'

'My dad says there's no point going to school if we're at war,' Clarence Cartwright concluded from the back of the classroom.

'There is always a point to school, Clarence, just remember that.' Ayda was firm but the questioning continued.

'Not if you're going to enlist like I am.'

'But, Billy, you're not even thirteen.' Ayda blinked, horrified, at the lanky lad sitting cross-legged in the front row. The class then began to fidget, the younger ones looking scared.

'Me dad says it won't matter; they'll need all the help they can get.' Billy Parker was now garnering looks of awe from the rest of the class.

'Guess it'll be a great lark! Better than working on the farm,' Thomas Smith, a thickset boy, remarked.

'Listen class, no one knows what's happening so, I suggest we forget about it, and concentrate on our letters and reading.'

Ayda hoped her cheerful tone would hide her own fear, but when Mrs Bellson and Mr Muir sat silhouetted against their newspapers, no one felt reassured.

By the beginning of August, a notice of closure hung at the school's entrance. Was it a sign of defiance or capitulation?

When Ayda returned to collect some possessions from the classroom, she heard muffled voices emanating from Mr Muir's study.

'Have you read about the Armenian crisis?'

'Oh, something's been grumbling, but I'm not sure of the detail.' Mrs Bellson's voice was a whisper.

'It's disgraceful. Bad enough the war in Europe, but the Turks have been rounding them up like cattle!'

'Rounding who up?'

'The Christians, ma'am.' Mr Muir sounded rattled. 'Dragging them over the border, starving then killing them. They're suspicious, that's why. Some are better educated: scientists, academics, so they're envious. And let me tell you something for nothing, it's been going on for years. *Years*!'

Feeling sick, Ayda dropped her books. She'd heard enough. Armenia was where her father lived, his homeland.

Outside, a crowd had gathered by another sign which read: *Medical Inspections*. Radlett had begun draining itself of its menfolk and the village had started to look empty. A chill crept down Ayda's spine.

Arriving at the Old Sheds, she saw Thomas wheeling out the 1909 Blériot XI, calmly draining oil from its Anzani engine. Adam was adjusting the Blackburn's warping wires, spinning a spanner between his fingers. Everything appeared normal: the fetor of fuel and fumes almost comforting as the two men tinkered around without a care. But, oddly, the machines looked vulnerable — more mosquito-like than ever, and this nagged at Ayda along with the rest of the week's troubles. School had been dismal but she felt safe here.

Adam turned to her. 'The situation abroad is changing day by day, Ayda. Father's kept a watchful eye on the Kaiser since July; but the news from the Foreign Office isn't good. Apparently, the Kaiser didn't take the assassination well — went very pale when told. Turns out he's one of the few who actually liked Archduke Franz. Been grief-stricken since so his response shouldn't surprise anyone.'

Her head really throbbed now.

'Ayda, you can't stay here as if nothing's happened. Have you thought about what you'll do? There's not much more we can teach you, and…' He hesitated. 'Thomas and I will be joining the R.F.C. In fact, we're leaving tomorrow for Upavon and training starts the day after. Sorry to shock you.' It was said very matter-of-factly, as if announcing a day out.

'I see.' Everything sounded definite, and she needed time to think.

'Listen, Ayda, I've been giving this a lot of thought. It would be a crying shame if your talents go unused — if you never fly again or end up in service … or worse.' Adam stood next to her, shaking his head like she was a problematic engine.

'But can't I teach?' Teaching *was* a respectable profession; one she'd adequately performed for over a year.

'Not if schools are closing everywhere,' he said. 'Soon you'll have to leave and travel to where your chances are better. Thomas has an aunt in north London who trains typists. We've made enquiries. She'll take you on, accommodate you. I've also paid for your Aero ticket at Hendon whenever you feel ready. You're good enough now, and you only need give my name.'

'But what use is a ticket if I can't join the R.F.C?'

'We'll see,' he said, looking away. 'I'm trying to arrange a few things. I still have to convince one or two people. Remember, Ayda, flying isn't just for war, there are other opportunities, trust me. It will put you in good stead, come what may.'

Well, what on earth did all that mean, she wondered?

Seeing her confusion, he smiled, cupping her face in his hands, lightly brushing her forehead. Thomas had finished the Blériot and was studying them, wiping his hands on a cloth.

'You'll be fine without us, Ayda, but I just need to give this to you.' Adam handed her an envelope. 'Be good. Think of us and keep things safe.'

Ayda felt like an outsider, understanding absolutely nothing.

Later, still feeling the touch of Adam's fingers on her face, she remembered his letter. Removing it, an awful gut-wrenching jealousy took hold of her. Adam and Thomas would get to fly in the R.F.C. and she wouldn't, even though she knew, of the three of them, she was the better pilot. 'But it's opportunity I want, not war,' she shouted at the room. She unfolded the letter.

Dear Ayda,

I would be grateful if we can leave plans for the Shuttle-Bound Mark 1 with you. You are a trusted friend and know you will keep everything safe. Can you also please check over our calculations, and make any adjustments? We are not happy with the overall drag coefficient but cannot see where to go from here. Sorry to ask, but who knows when we'll next avail ourselves of your excellent brain?

Your friend,

Adam

P.S. Delighted with any recommendations you see fit to make.

She looked around the cottage for the plans. There was something under the door: a large, manila envelope had caught on its rough under-surface. The sketches inside showed errors: heat capacities not reflecting the materials, thrust overcompensated for. After a quick adjustment, the drawings were pushed back inside — they'd be much happier now, she thought, wondering when she'd see Adam and Thomas again. Being part of a team, listened to, treated as an equal made her heart sing almost as much as flying did. Then a tiny white square floated to the ground: a smaller note in bold lettering which must have been enclosed with the drawings: *REMEMBER HENDON, MENTION ME!*

Hendon? But her mind was focussed on London, and the war. Disturbance, change, on the move again like before with her mother. Rosina washing, ironing, cleaning somewhere new — her standing, watching, alone with numbers in her head for company. Again. She had thought she belonged here, found something she could do well, something she *loved* — with Adam, with Thomas, the planes. Now this war meant everything slipping through her fingers like water.

Stop it. One thing at a time, she thought, giving herself a mental shake and pushing the note firmly back inside the envelope. She realised she needed to have one final conversation before leaving — one that she was dreading.

Ayda's relationship with her mother had deteriorated from the day she had discovered her birth certificate. Working at the school and visiting the Old Sheds meant they rarely saw each other, but this war had brought things to a head. Soon, she would be heading to London, to a new career and, hopefully, to fly. And whatever she felt about her mother, she needed to be told. But how would she make her *understand*?

The following day, Ayda found Rosina on the front lawn with Lady Clarissa. She was shocked by Lady Clarissa's appearance: hollow-eyed and gaunt. Seeing Ayda's face, Lady Clarissa wobbled back along the garden path, clinging to the fence and leaving Ayda alone with her mother.

'Mama, I am leaving for London,' Ayda whispered. 'This war means I cannot stay here. And I want to fly.' She waited, watching her mother's brow furrow, seeing if she had understood.

'*Cara mia. Una professione.* You promise me — good job — teacher. *Che cosa* flying?'

Ayda grasped her mother's hand. '*Pilota donna,* mama. *Capisci?* An aviatrix!'

Squeezing Ayda's hand, Rosina's face lit up. '*Si, si. Capisco. Molto bene,* Ayda!'

For a moment, they stood looking at each other, Ayda basking in her mother's praise. It was enough. And it meant a lot.

Watching her mother retrace Lady Clarissa's steps, Ayda felt satisfied. But now she had to get to London, learn a new skill, find a new home, take her Royal Aero Club ticket, all without Adam and Thomas, and all before she would be allowed to fly. And flying was the easy bit.

CHAPTER 9

Ayda had visited many places, but none were like London.

A mass of people rushed around her. Smog-filled streets crammed the capital, ugly block buildings, terraces, all ringing with a cacophony of noises she didn't recognise. With barely any green compared to Hertfordshire, the motor cars and omnibuses were a mechanic's dream, and she wondered what Thomas would have made of them.

Her journey from Hertfordshire had been rushed with barely time to pack or bid goodbye to her mother, who she doubted understood all that was going on. Finally, she was standing in Ealing Broadway at the foot of a steep staircase that would lead to her new employment. She paused, smoothing down her wayward hair, steeling herself as her legs wobbled up the stone steps. At the first-floor room, a mechanical click-clacking noise grew louder before being drowned out by the staccato sound of heels on floorboards. The door then swung open.

'Just in time. You must be Miss Gulzar?'

Ayda followed her through the door and found twenty pairs of eyes staring at her reddened face. Since discovering her birth certificate, she had been determined to change her name, but now wished it was less conspicuous.

'You're not late yet, though you do cut it fine.'

The woman's elongated fingers indicated a front row desk into which Ayda obediently fell and she introduced her to Miss Brace, the supervisor.

Miss Brace hovered, plying paper into Ayda's typewriter. After instructions on technique, position of keys and layout, she departed and the room typed on oblivious. Ayda waited for her return, then glanced left then right; both her neighbours were bent low over their typewriters, their fingers gliding over the keys. There was nothing for it, and with her own fingers rapidly cooling, she loaded more paper, and began to type. Her progress was slow — unlike her flying.

For the next hour, Miss Brace patrolled the aisles, her ponderous gait giving fair warning of her approach. By the second hour, Ayda had settled into a solid rhythm — not thinking, imagining or problem solving, her letter pile slowly reducing and, save for the clock's chimes and the clacking of keys all around her, she typed on in silence until luncheon, and thereafter for a further six hours.

At 6 p.m. a bell sounded. Stiff and relieved, Ayda looked up. The two figures either side of her, were now in front of her desk, one even holding out her hand.

'Mabel's the name,' the young woman said, a faint smile on her lips. 'Been told we're to take you to the flat.'

'Flat?' Ayda said. 'Oh yes, of course. The flat, my lodgings in Acton Town. That would be very helpful — you see, I'm new to London and only have an address.' She unfurled a scrap of paper, aware of another pair of eyes on her. The second woman, the taller of the two, had folded her arms and was watching before finally speaking.

'From the country, aren't ya? Thought we better show you where to go. After all, we're all gonna be living together.'

Now it was Ayda's turn to stare. 'We are?'

Mabel patted her tight red curls. 'There are eight of us in our lodgings, including Velma here, all of us typists. Miss Brace likes us all in together, says that way we can look out for one another.'

Velma folded her arms even tighter. 'That's because she don't trust us. Any of us. Anyways, we better get off, place'll be all locked up like a jail at half past the hour.'

Soon the three of them were outside on the street under a blanket of sky, and heading from the office towards their lodgings, Ayda glad to have survived her first day — tomorrow would be better, she was sure. But despite the hour's walk outdoors, she hadn't managed to rid her nostrils of the office's dampness and coal-choked chimney. Still, the pristine chimneys of her new Edwardian lodgings smelled fresh by comparison and she gulped the clean air deep into her lungs. Leafy trees swayed over the terraces, and rows of carefully tended gardens full of shrubs and bedding plants, made it look pretty.

Inside was a different matter though. The *new* not applying to the third floor where she was taken. A gloomy corridor of bald, badly furnished rooms stretched out in front of her, each bedroom housing four beds, a double wardrobe, and a sink in the corner. At the far end, a bathroom with a wheezing geyser and water closet completed the accommodation. Meals were to be taken downstairs, and all for the princely sum of a shilling per week, which, Ayda knew, was good value for London. But there were no shelves, and nowhere for her books. Forcing a smile, she turned to a beaming Mabel.

'Happy?'

'Why yes, of course,' she lied.

But as the weeks passed, she made little headway getting to know the other typists. All were respectable, hardworking young women and some, including Velma, were quick and bright, although her mathematical ability was barely above elementary. But none felt passionately about anything except their menfolk, and work was viewed as something to pass the time until the war was over. None considered it a vocation or a career or even interesting. Ayda couldn't really blame them, for the work they did was tedious: lists or letters, and occasionally fundraising leaflets for local women's groups all supporting the men at war, and she couldn't help feeling that in a world without ambition, women were becoming even more invisible. So, on she typed, listening to their talk, numbing herself to conversation or thought, knowing only that the things they wanted were not the things she did.

Trudging back to her lodgings one evening a few months later, a humorous painted postcard waited for her: the Kaiser Bill. With the world in his mouth, his upturned pointy moustache almost made her laugh, but on a gloomy November evening, laughter felt out of place and the words on the back were suitably sobering:

I am keeping well. Visited some beautiful woods recently and have sent you a memento of war.

Please remember me.

Adam

Days later, a crumpled envelope arrived from Adam. It was sent from Sanctuary Wood in Ypres. She removed the piece of dried lavender that was inside and let out a long sigh. It was only a memento, but it reminded her of the two friends she desperately missed. She pictured fields of mauve amidst the red carnage, noticing that her cheeks were damp. She missed Adam and Thomas, her old life, St Theresa's — even her mother. There she had a home and she missed it, and her dream of flying — which was just that. A dream.

And on this dismal London evening, the war seemed even more remote and mysterious as the Londoners carried on much as before, but without their menfolk. Nobody talked much about it, though the newspapers were awash with updates. Many considered the war would be finished by Christmas, and everything would return to normal, and little by little, the monotony of Ayda's life sucked her into this fantasy.

During luncheon, someone might mention a letter, and she would gaze at her piece of lavender wondering when she would receive news. It smelled how lavender should smell: faint, warm, with a light scent fading like a gentle breeze. Thinking of Adam, of Thomas, she wondered how war was treating them as her days and months of typing crept by, numbing her mind and spirit. At night, the *plink, plink* sound of a typewriter never left her, dulling her mind, stupefying her brain.

She would often think of her father, too, wondering which war he was fighting. Occasionally, Adam's words would drift back: *REMEMBER HENDON, MENTION ME!* Then she would forget again, scared of uncertainty or whether Hendon even *wanted* her. Doubts crept in. Could she really summon up the courage to walk into Hendon Aerodrome, a woman alone, and fly without Adam and Thomas, now that typing a few letters was all that she did with her days?

As Christmas 1914 came and went with no letters from France, the war continued, and Ayda doubted whether her friends even thought of her anymore. Adam and Thomas would be risking their lives, but at least they would be outside flying under the sky, and she knew she would join them in a heartbeat given the chance. And as the months passed by, the effort of convincing anyone at Hendon of her worth seemed insurmountable. So it was simple. She wouldn't.

PART 2

CHAPTER 10

3rd March 1915, Merville, France

Captain Adam Bound stared up over a row of canvas tents as five spidery machines came into view. Eyeing the sky as the rhythmic humming increased, his boots rearranged the mess carpet — then he heard a splutter — the nearest machine had misfired into a howling tailspin. A few pilots drifted outside to watch but most held their breath and waited. Luckily, the machine righted itself, and the relief was palpable.

'Jolly good show,' Lieutenant Giles Devenport said, shoving a billiards cue at Adam. 'Care to play?'

'Not right now, the tender's expected,' he said, skirting round the cue. '"C" Flight needs debriefing, assuming they can land safely, but I say, that tailspin's really put the wind up.'

'Quite!' Lieutenant John Hastings agreed, surveying the men around him. Devenport had joined 2nd Lieutenant Connor Murphy and the two were hunched over a chess board, while Captain Thomas Beauly of 'B' Flight sat cross-legged on a couch smoking a pipe, a banjo propped against him.

'Expecting many?' Hastings asked.

'Eh?' Adam said, still watching 'C' Flight's B.E.2's bouncing across the airfield.

'The tender, you know, the new recruits? Are you expecting many?'

'Just the one.'

Adam had been with 39a Squadron at Merville ten miles southeast of St Omer for five months now. Of its sixty men, half were pilots, the rest mechanics, cooks, armoury or intelligence officers, as well as one padre. Barely alone since he started, the squadron had become Adam's family, his true family. The men were like brothers and he experienced a camaraderie he'd never known before.

Glancing at the tents flapping in the breeze, he suddenly felt anxious and very protective of them, for in the last six weeks, every newcomer at 39a had lasted no more than five days, the most recent, a lad from Helensburgh, surviving only two.

Since the beginning of 1915, the war had metamorphosed into something evil. While training at the Central Flying School in Wiltshire, talk was always of the chivalry that existed between pilots on *both* sides: a careful nod, an acknowledgement, a courteous wave that said they were above the carnage. Not anymore. Things had turned decidedly nasty. Pilots on both sides were now fighting like the poor sods on the ground, hoping to inflict maximum damage. And at 39a, something else was happening, something that wasn't just down to bad luck…

On arrival, all the recruits had spent their first few hours sitting around the piano. But one chair in particular, an old leather dining chair, had become notorious. Each new recruit who sat in it had been killed the next day: three had been shot down on their first flight, one was hit by ground fire, two by a nearby enemy squadron, and another two had crashed after developing engine trouble. Now no one sat in the red dining chair, with most men refusing to even touch it. Adam knew this was ridiculous — outrageous even, as he always put faith in science rather than superstition, but facts were facts. His first instinct had been to burn the chair and he'd been about to do just that, when he had been stopped.

'Don't touch it, sir!' Murphy had cried, pulling him away from it.

Adam was interrupted from making a decision about the chair by the surprise of the new arrival.

Standing over six feet tall, the man's body was held up by matchstick legs, and Adam took a step back at the intensity of the deep-set blue eyes raking over him. The stranger extended a bony hand, while the corners of his mouth upturned, giving the impression of smugness and superiority. The man looked older than everyone around him, closer to thirty than twenty.

'You must be Captain Bound. Second Lieutenant Randal, sir, Rick Randal.'

'Good show, Randal, glad to have you on board. Make yourself at home.' Adam grasped the proffered hand with vigour as Randal inclined his large head, slipping his other hand onto the red dining chair.

'Best not sit there,' Hastings said, kicking it away.

Randal turned his penetrating eyes on Hastings, before picking up his kit bag, and sloping off.

'I say, he's a friendly one,' Hastings muttered, sarcastically.

'Probably won't last the week,' Adam replied.

Pessimism had never come naturally to Adam, but the war had changed that.

Randal was quickly forgotten, as 'C' Flight gathered round their captain for de-briefing. They were one short. Graham Barker, their latest addition, hadn't returned from the flight. Bad luck from the red dining chair? Deep down, Adam knew luck had little to do with it. It had a lot more to do with insufficient training.

Men were arriving without the minimum fifteen hours flying training, the attitude being to just get them to the front as fast as possible. Unless things changed, the squadron would be bled dry before long.

Taking a deep breath, Adam prepared to talk, but he was at a loss over what to say. How the dickens could he make his men feel good, when all he had were negative thoughts swirling through his head. He was desperate for leave, or even just one undisturbed night's sleep, a chance to relax and map the night sky in peace.

Here, life revolved around flights with analyses on performance — had they kept formation, or engaged with the enemy when needed? And half the time, he just didn't know, believing that sometimes it *did* come down to luck; skill was involved too — if you couldn't handle your bus or got the wind up, then you were probably a dead man, though luck often determined whether you were in the wrong place at the wrong time, or if your guns seized, or engine misfired. He wondered what would happen if he just told the truth, that sometimes things went wrong because the men were frightened, or because they had been given bad information, or for no clear reason at all. His role was to sound enthusiastic, to encourage his flight, but how could he when men were dying all around him?

He glanced at his letter pile, feeling sick, mentally adding Barker to it. After five months, he was none the wiser on how to phrase the terrible telegrams to the families. *Dear Mr and Mrs, it is with regret*, or the more direct: *Your son has been shot down*, were the current favourites, but they sounded so cold and impersonal. He couldn't imagine they would bring any comfort to a grieving mother or widow.

He couldn't remember when he'd last written a cheerful letter, or one to his friend, Ayda. All around him, men wrote to their sweethearts, fiancées, wives — never to a female friend. It made him feel childish, but what else was Ayda? Someone he admired; someone intelligent, capable, who appreciated him, though he also found her attractive… He wondered what she was doing now. Probably typing letters, and likely more pleasant ones than he was.

CHAPTER 11

Adam was right: Ayda had been spending her time typing. At the start of the year, Ayda got a minor typing role at the War Office. She'd been grateful for the move. Although the work was tedious for the most part, every now and then she stumbled across something interesting. Her first job this morning was to type out the diary of one Private William Mackay, a 2nd Battalion Seaforth Highlander. She couldn't understand why she'd been asked to do such a thing, but it was heart-breaking. She worked nonstop until lunchtime to finish the project, and it was only when she got to the very end of the diary, she realised why she'd been asked to transcribe it. A small official note was glued onto the end piece informing William's family that he'd been shot, not in the line of duty, but by an execution squad.

The diary had been split into three entries. William's words swam from her fingers into her heart, each entry more harrowing and more poignant.

24th April 1915

2 p.m.

I am allowed a visitor, and Robertson has now visited. His spirits are high, his injuries minor and he has heard rumours of the new C.O. Apparently, he was in the Canadian outback before meeting with the Canadian Seaforth Highlanders in Vancouver. When their help at the war's start was refused, he joined the 2nd Battalion training with them, rising through the ranks. I'm told he is English, yet rumours are that his face is badly scarred, either from a bear, a moose or a wolf, and that he has the look of a hunted animal about him. I'd be lying if I said I wasn't a wee bit worried but the man can't help his looks, can he? Relieving 'C' Company expected soon.

5 p.m.

It is done now. My fate is sealed. Sergeant Kilbride tried, he really did.

'Listen, sir, I'm nae condoning his actions, but the boy's a fool,' I heard him saying to the C.O. 'Not right in the head since we were all gassed, sir. He's just a wee boy, too damn soft, an innocent.'

Then I chanced a long, hard look at the C.O. And the rumours weren't wrong.

A gaping red wound ran across his scarred forehead giving him the look of animal prey. His cropped hair the colour of midnight clung to his pale white skin. His eyes, deep-set in bony sockets, as dark as night and as distant, sent shivers down my spine. He has wired all the way through to General Haig who concluded I should have followed orders. And the C.O., that is Captain Granville Bound, came to see me afterwards looking pleased with himself. I thought he would set me free. Not a hope! Then he looked at me with those eyes; glazed, boring through to my very soul, rubbing at his scar till it wept red and twitched, and then he said as calm as anything: 'I cannot abide disobedience in my unit no matter what. You should be taught a lesson Mackay. I think you know your punishment?'

Forgive me for saying, but I damned Captain Granville to hell for what he said, the way he spoke to me. Please believe me when I say I am innocent, that I have committed no crime, hurt no one.

6 p.m.

I await the tender. I have seen the padre. He has explained things to me, and I am content. I know my fate. I will be sent back to Poperinge.

I can picture the thick wooden post now jutting from the centre, the shadows menacing along the floor. I didn't know what it was for then. No one talked about it — there was no need. I know now: twelve soldiers with guns. One blank.

The light is fading fast, and I see the post again. A white cloth is to be pinned over my heart. I will refuse a blindfold — for I have done no wrong, I will look each one of them in the eye and pray they can live with themselves.

Goodbye Father, Mother, little Callum, little Ciorstaidh, darling Bessie, mo ghaol. Forget me and marry well. Know that I go to the Almighty innocent and that I love you all. May this diary bear witness.

William Duncan Mackay, 24th April 1915

At lunchtime, red-eyed and ashen, Ayda headed for a nearby tearoom. She was armed with a newspaper, reasoning that even newsprint had to be more cheerful than transcripts from dead soldiers. And she was right. Halfway down she saw it — in the announcements. The muscles on her face immediately relaxed — she was actually smiling.

11th August 1915

Capt. Adam Prendergast Gervaise Bound R.F.C. awarded the Military Cross for conspicuous gallantry and devotion to duty. While on patrol he attacked at close range two hostile machines, both of which stalled and fell sideways. Shortly afterwards, he attacked two more, both were sent down out of control. On three more occasions he flew over the lines at about 75 feet attacking enemy balloons, bringing one down in flames.

Sipping her tea, she started feeling better. *The Telegraph* was spread out in front of her as she read of Adam's award, knowing he'd soon be on leave, wondering if the war had changed him. His letters had been infrequent and she hoped she would at least recognise him — but maybe she had changed too? After twelve months, she would soon be attaching a face to her old friend.

She finished her lunch and trudged back to the vast neo-Baroque War Office. The trapezium-shaped structure still overwhelmed her, spreading its shadows across the streets of Whitehall like ink clouding water. Her work was becoming more disturbing as the months went on, often tugging at her heartstrings as she typed about real people and real problems.

At 1.30 p.m., Ayda approached her office, knowing another diary was waiting for her. This diary was shorter, a small, leather-bound book with staining across its spine. It looked more like a ledger, or something Adam would have kept to record his scientific findings. Looking closer, she noticed the entries were recent, starting from only a month previously.

10th August 1915
Suvla Beach, north of Anzac Cove
10 a.m.

In the four months we Royal Engineers have been here, things have got worse. Life is a struggle, with dust, searing heat, and a severe shortage of water coming only via mules in cans from supply ships. Flies are a challenge too, smothering every scrap of food, giving us all dysentery, making settling here in the Gallipoli peninsula impossible. But today is a good day. Finally, an interlude in the fighting. The M.O. was pleased with my sunstroke sores and I have good news (I hope) in the form of a letter (from Manchester). I am confident it is from Ernest and if I can only fix this infernal echo in my mouthpiece, I may be afforded half an hour's peace to read it. Oh, the toils of a signals officer!

11 a.m.

My letter is detailed, and is indeed from Dr Ernest Rutherford on University of Manchester paper. He brings good tidings, that Richard has been awarded the Nobel. I am very happy for him so have added a formal notification here:

Nobel Prize for Chemistry awarded to Richard Martin Willstatter, director of the Kaiser Wilhelm Institute for Chemistry, for the study of the structure of pigments of flowers and fruits, and for showing that chlorophyll is a mixture of chlorophyll a and b isomers.

It is well deserved. How long ago it seems since we met along with Fritz Haber at Neptune Hall, all of us on holiday. Much has happened since. I am so grateful they stumbled on our little scientific meeting, and stayed a short while. Often, I wonder what they would have made of Livens' flame projector, and as peacemakers, both would have been deeply disturbed. Ernest mentions Richard was asked to develop poisonous gases for the war effort, but declined in order to work on clothing protection instead. I was right. He is a true peacemaker!

Noon

Duty calls. There is disturbance from the Turkish trench ten yards behind, and I may have to telephone through my orders. But no, I think they are back under cover. I am grateful to ponder my correspondence a while longer despite the cruel midday sun.

But I am so thirsty, and cannot remember when I last had water. All around, the corpses lie festering, the sand dunes dancing before my eyes.

It is strange to think I only feel admiration for my colleague and fellow scientist, Richard, and hope if it were me as the recipient of the Nobel, he would think the same. So glad that the science of Chemistry lives on despite the carnage so perhaps our luck may change soon?

12.15 p.m.

It is upon us again. I have received orders

The diary stopped abruptly. As Ayda typed the words up, she knew her earlier apprehension had been well-founded. A twisting sensation at the pit of her stomach made her nauseous. She had been present that day at Neptune Hall, watching from the outside, maybe she had seen this poor soldier then? Desperately running through the speakers — she wondered who he could be? Adam, she remembered, had been particularly impressed by another young scientist. As if to answer, a thin wisp of newsprint fell out from behind the diary. With a sinking heart, she read the obituary:

At 5 p.m. on 10th August 1915, Henry Gwyn Jeffreys Moseley lay where he fell, a single bullet between his eyes. He was just 27 years old, yet another victim of the Battle of Gallipoli. The Turkish sniper did not live long afterwards, apparently one of Mustafa Kemal's best, but only the second best to fall that day.

Moseley's Law provided a natural explanation for the way the elements are organised in the Periodic Table, leading Moseley to predict the existence of several elements, one investigated whilst in Gallipoli. His work on the structure of the so-called atom, although controversial, was thought to be in line for next year's Nobel Prize for Chemistry. His premature death was not just bad luck but a complete travesty. His first paper was received in July 1913 with great interest, a subsequent paper was given y at Neptune Hall, Elstree in October 1913.

She had been there. Reading of the death of Henry Moseley was the final straw. No longer could she go on reliving these men's last moments, no matter how noble, brave or selfless they had been, she could not cope with their pain. Their war had weaved its way into her heart and mind so that she could no longer hide her tears from the other typists. She felt for these men, cared for them as their tragic stories brutally unfolded before her in black and white, and it was tearing her apart.

Flying was the key — the escape. She didn't want to waste any more time typing.

Stepping inside an aircraft always made her forget *any* problem, so why had she left it so long? Next week she would see Adam. She would need to explain herself, explain why she still hadn't got her ticket. His words from over a year ago crept back: *REMEMBER HENDON, MENTION ME!* She hoped he wouldn't be too disappointed in her for not taking his advice sooner.

A week later Ayda was waiting nervously on the Strand when a pale uniformed figure with a feathery moustache approached her and soon Adam's arms were warm around her. No, she thought, relieved, Adam hadn't changed. They met in the opulent surroundings of the Savoy where gold fleur-de-lys scrolls sat walled above mahogany panels. They were shown to their table which was near the grand piano where a Chopin Nocturne was being played. Above them, a stained-glass dome fanned a kaleidoscope of colours in every direction. Gazing upwards, Ayda was reminded of a planetarium, the black crystal chandelier casting a sultry ambience as black-tailed uniforms worked the floor, taking orders and bringing afternoon tea or champagne.

'Marvellous to see you, Ayda, you do look well,' Adam said, taking her hand.

'As do you.'

They waited awkwardly while a waitress poured tea and placed biscuits on the table, then, leaning forwards, Adam broke the silence.

'I'm so pleased you could come today, Ayda. I've got some fantastic news — here!' He slipped a note across the table. 'A decision's been reached. Captain Bonneville, Central Flying School — he'll be your contact.'

Ayda stared, confused, before seeing her name and address on the note.

'I've told them all about you,' Adam continued. 'Made them realise your worth. It's gone to the top and back down again. Father's got involved too. All hush-hush and top secret, you understand, but make no mistake, it's usually only men used for this type of work, but we're going out on a limb for you because you're different.'

Across the table, Ayda was watching him closely, stirring her tea, the teaspoon rattling against the side of her cup.

'For what type of work, Adam? I'm sorry, but I don't really understand...'

'Of course you do,' he said, thrusting himself up in his seat. 'I've spent the last year working on Father, and let me tell you, it hasn't been easy! The Central Flying School is in Upavon, they need delivery pilots to collect planes from the feeder flying schools into the Central. We need more pilots, more mechanics, just like you. You'll start by flying B.E.2 crates from the Royal Aircraft Factory in Farnborough. B.E.2 stands for Blériot Experimental, and you'll be responsible for their basic maintenance, too. You'll probably have to fly with very little notice, but remember, this is *secret*. No one must know, do you understand?'

Finally, the penny dropped. He was telling her that her dream of flying was about to come true. Head reeling, she grabbed the sides of her chair.

Unaware of her shock, Adam continued. 'They'll examine you first, probably at Farnborough. Make sure you're the ticket. The military never take anything for granted. But speaking of tickets, you simply must get yours, this can't happen without it!'

Smiling inanely, Ayda found she could just about speak and stammered a reply.

'This is such wonderful news, Adam. Thank you so, so much. I really cannot believe it!'

'Pleased then?'

'Oh yes! This means the world to me.'

'Then what were you playing at, Ayda? Why have you spent so long typing? I am truly puzzled.'

Her colour rose sharply. 'Well, typing wouldn't be my first choice of occupation, but, in the circumstances I…' She trailed off, feeling flustered, and reached for a glass of water.

Adam was smirking. 'I just fail to comprehend how someone with such flying ability and intelligence can spend so long typing inconsequential letters for Lady La-di-dah's Socks-for-Troops Sewing Circle, or some such tosh!'

Leaning back in the velvet chair, her flush deepened. 'It wasn't all like that. I was working for the War Office. It felt important.' But she knew he was right; why had she carried on with it for so long?

'Really, Ayda! What I'm trying to say is that you should be using your talents. Did you perhaps forget you could fly?'

'Well, perhaps I did just a bit. You see, I didn't want to get my hopes up, then be disappointed. I honestly didn't believe anything could be done for me, and thought if I did something worthwhile, it would be enough. But lately, at the War Office, it's been … harrowing, and now, I would really welcome a change.'

Across the table, Adam muttered, 'Harrowing is right, my dear,' but when she looked up, he was smiling.

'Now that you've assured me you haven't forgotten about flying, I have to tell you they've recognised that you're one of kind, but still, there's something you must understand. This really *is* secret. Women do not fly military aircraft. No one must know.'

'No one?'

'No one.' He stood up and planted a kiss on her cheek. 'Congratulations, Ayda. I'm sure you're going to love your new role.'

'But, Adam,' she said, alarmed, 'you haven't told me your news, what you've be doing — the war.' She grabbed his hands, feeling stricken. Surely, he couldn't be leaving now? There was so much she had planned to say.

A shadow fell over his face, his smile vanishing into it. 'It can wait for another time. The trouble is, I had a wire this morning, my leave's been cut short, things are hotting up again, and I've to report back as soon as possible. Can't do without me, I guess.'

'But you've hardly been back at all.'

His gaze, she saw, wasn't as steady as before, his manner not as relaxed, and she was sure his legs were trembling. What was he was hiding? Casting her mind back to her most recent transcripts, she had a good idea.

'My leave was just shy of one week. And my presence is required at home too, worse luck!' But his smile was now firmly back in place. 'Still, I've done what I needed to, and I had to tell you personally — you understand. Goodbye, Ayda.'

He really was leaving now.

'Don't worry, I'll see myself home.'

It didn't matter, he'd gone already, and he'd told her nothing about his war. She knew no more about Captain Adam Bound, flying in 39a Squadron, than she had that morning, except that Adam liked secrets too.

CHAPTER 12

On Friday, 24th September 1915, Ayda arrived at Hendon Aerodrome to join the Ruffy-Baumann Flying School. At reception she was told the quota was filled. She cleared her throat.

'I heard you were accepting civilians.'

The rotund man in the main reception looked her up and down.

'Look, miss. The military comes first, that is the R.N.A.S. and the R.F.C. May I suggest the Ewen if you are looking for a bunt?'

Ayda looked wearily at the smirking face.

'I don't want a bunt, sir, or a jaunt, I'd like to fl—'

'Ah, there's a lot we'd all like to do, young miss, but there's a war on. And pilots for war are the priority.'

She felt close to giving up. Flying came so easily to her, but here they were making it difficult.

'My friend said everything was arranged,that I only had to—'

'Try the Grahame-White. They might take you both up for a spin. Maybe take a picnic — they'll let you make a day of it if you pay them well enough.'

The clerk chuckled to himself then closed the door in her face.

Outside, she started to walk away, but then she saw uniformed men performing their prescribed circuits and injustice welled up inside of her. She decided the time for meek acceptance had gone. Unless she stood up for herself, made herself heard, nothing would change and she might just as well go back to typing. She absolutely *needed* her Aero Ticket to fly.

She took a deep breath and pushed the door open again. Before the incredulous clerk could open his mouth, she explained she was here to fulfil a pre-arranged appointment made by her friend, Captain Adam Bound, of 39a Squadron — son of Lord Gervaise Bound — grandee of the War Office.

A stillness engulfed the reception area as the clerk looked at her, dumbfounded.

Within minutes, she was adjusting the strap of a standard issue flying helmet, stepping into the smallest jacket and salopettes the stores possessed. A single name had elicited the change: *Bound.*

A Caudron G3 was wheeled out. She felt a mixture of nerves and euphoria, and yes, it really did resemble a copper bathtub on wheels, but she didn't care. She thought it beautiful. Eyes searching, she studied the controls, feeling the plane, getting to know it, delighting in the smell of castor oil as if it was an expensive French scent.

Propeller turning, the eighty-horsepower Le Rhône engine sprung to life as she shouted 'Contact,' and, trembling from head to toe — from joy, not fear, she advanced the little plane along the grass. It was like being reunited with a long-lost friend and she made her decision there and then that she would never stop flying again.

Take-off complete, air/fuel mixture adjusted, Ayda judged full throttle was at twelve hundred revolutions. In the sky, the air felt thinner, cleaner and still warm. At two hundred feet, the Hendon circuit with its redbrick buildings and green oval retreated from view and she forced herself to concentrate not luxuriate.

Completing her two distance flights of around four miles with ease, Ayda would have continued further, higher, but remembered this was a test, and not the time or place for showing off. Finishing her turns, changing direction and producing several figures of eight, tears blurred her vision. It was almost over. Hitting the kill-switch on the control stick and running her engine wide open, she reluctantly turned back, controlling her speed and by the time the G3 came to rest within the stipulated 164-foot mark, she was calm enough that she knew she wouldn't cry again.

A small crowd had gathered and someone helped her down, others patted her on the back, a few asking how many times she'd flown a Caudron.

At reception, the rotund clerk stood in front of the desk nodding as the typist behind abandoned her typewriter to congratulate Ayda.

Ayda had been given Aero Ticket 1622. The Royal Aero Club now officially considered her to be a pilot. Relieved and overjoyed, she sent a silent thank you to her friend, Adam Bound.

Despite the need for non-combat or ground pilots, Ayda wasn't summoned by Captain Bonneville until early 1916. By then, she had reluctantly returned to the War Office, grateful a place was still available so she could earn enough to pay her rent. At last, the news came that at 0700 hours on 2nd April 1916, she would be required to deliver a D.H.2 to Farnborough for repair. Sixty miles of careful flying. It was a start.

Her balloon-shaped overalls, sheepskin boots and jacket were hanging ready when she arrived, but her joy felt somewhat muted for Adam was not there to share the moment with her. Could she really do this; deliver and service aeroplanes? She pictured the bolted door at Neptune Hall and the smirking clerk shutting the door in her face at Hendon. At last, one door had opened, and unless she barged through it and seized the opportunity, she might find it closed again or taken away. This job was the first step into her future.

But not everyone at Farnborough was happy to see her there. By the end of her first week, a familiar pattern had begun to emerge. Every time she heard: 'Pilots, go to your plane', a fault was discovered on her aircraft. After days of faulty spark plugs, tainted fuel, and even a split carburettor, Ayda had had enough.

'Sir, yet again, it appears my B.E.2 has problems,' she said on the final day of her first week.

The assessor feigned surprise. 'Well, well! Poor Miss Gulzar has another problem. Gather round please.'

Six pairs of eyes focussed on her, making Ayda feel ambushed. The assessor's thread-like lips soon broke the silence.

'Miss Gulzar, a ground pilot must be a mechanic as well. Often you will be on your own and I have to be certain you can manage. Now, kindly rectify your plane's fault. You have ten minutes. If not, the tearoom needs waiting staff and it may be that you will find a more suitable position there.'

An older pilot in his fifties coughed, throwing her a sympathetic look. Walking to her B.E.2, she shot the assessor a cold look, her heart hammering in her chest. No! He would not triumph. This mattered too much. And no! She would *not* be belittled.

'Of course, sir.'

She had noticed a leaking gasket. Willing her clammy fingers to work, she carefully removed something from behind the gasket.

'Sir, this gasket is leaking, reducing the engine's compression ratio. I would seal it but there seems to be a foreign item here. I believe this sheet belongs to you?'

His glare couldn't diminish her smile as she handed him a screwed-up assessment sheet.

'Well, Miss Gulzar,' he said, snatching it. 'I suppose I must offer my congratulations. You are indeed a competent pilot and mechanic, worthy of accreditation.'

She was finally handed a certificate with *Ferry Pilot 13* stamped across it, but the assessor hadn't finished.

'Make no mistake,' he warned, face flushed, 'you are a civilian assisting in times of war. You are *not* a pilot of the R.F.C. There are no women pilots in the R.F.C.' The statement was spat at her, but by now she had worked out why — fear. If women took *all* the ground jobs from men, then they might be called up to the frontlines, even this assessor. And not every man welcomed that, she realised, looking around at her colleagues, who were busy welcoming Britain's only female dispatch pilot.

Two weeks later the day of Ayda's first dispatch finally arrived. The plane sat waiting on the grass, fuelled, its wings and struts fluttering in the breeze. Ayda had been expecting a B.E.2 but was delighted to see the curved, tub-like cockpit of a D.H.2, a plane she knew intimately and had flown with Adam at the Old Sheds. A cluster of men with time on their hands had gathered to watch and she played along, giving them a bow.

Take-off from the Central was a near perfect affair, but now it was time to concentrate. Engine handling in a D.H.2 was simple: no mixture control, no carburettor heat, or fixed pitch prop. At one thousand feet, the rear rotary pusher engine purred its approval as she sat hugged inside its cockpit.

Chancing a look over the side, her feelings overwhelmed her. The speed. The wind. The beauty of the view.

At nearly 100 mph, the earth sped past in all its scenic detail and with sixty miles of adventure ahead of her, the need for careful navigation was important. Her route had been meticulously planned for there was nothing more demeaning than for a pilot to admit they were lost and have to ask for directions. But today's route was more roundabout than she was used to. It wound over the Sussex Downs via Winchester, taking in its magnificent cathedral before turning south towards the massive Farnborough site.

Spread over miles of Hampshire countryside, the Farnborough factory employed over four thousand individuals, who worked night and day producing and repairing aircraft. Surrounded by a cluster of trees, it boasted towering vertical hangars, the tallest of them housing the Gamma airships with their strange bulbous shapes.

After forty-five minutes, the hangars became visible and Farnborough's chalky white landing area blurred through the mist and haze. Ayda picked her approach into the wind, reducing power to give a steady descent of sixty knots. The D.H.2 liked this, and at thirty feet, she gently eased her rate of descent again, slowly rotating to almost level at fifteen feet, and bouncing and flying at around forty knots. After about a hundred yards of ground rolling, she continued with a touch of full rudder and the odd burst of power, and managed not to swing around too much.

Perfect.

The final part had her taxiing towards yet another batch of men who were avidly watching. A bushy-haired man as wide as he was tall, edged through the landing party, holding out his hand.

'Captain Bonneville,' he announced gruffly, engulfing her in a bear-like hug once she had exited the plane. 'Delighted to meet you at last, my dear. We're hearing great things about you, Ayda.' He waved at a line of D.H.2's before removing a white envelope from his pocket.

'Your orders for the next week,' he said. 'We're truly grateful for your assistance, but there's much to do. Any problems, let me know, I'm usually at the Central but today I wanted to welcome you here personally.' He gave her hand another squeeze before scurrying towards a newly started D.H.2, then calling back, 'Please give Captain Bound my heartfelt thanks.'

Ayda let out a relieved sigh. Her first day as a pilot was complete and things were looking up. At last.

CHAPTER 13

Six weeks later, Adam was on leave again and had invited Ayda to join him at The London Pavilion in Piccadilly Circus.

A lone tenor's voice rose above the music hall's laughter and boom from the brass band.

In the dining area, Adam and Ayda were sitting across from each other.

'Thanks awfully for asking me here. It's lovely — really it is,' she said.

Adam's face looked pinched and drawn, unrecognisable from their last meeting at the Savoy. Although Ayda was bursting with her own news, she wanted to let him lead the conversation, so, settling back, she waited.

Adam smiled. 'I'm sorry, Ayda, I appear to have forgotten my manners, and the art of conversation.'

Ayda's eyes widened as he wrestled with his thoughts, their conversation stalling again. There was no buoyancy, humour, or spirit about him. That he had changed so much in seven months shocked her. Even speaking was an effort for him.

The brass band packed away their trumpets and saxophones while she waited, a small orchestra now beginning its dramatic first piece: a slightly threatening sound filling the hall as the drums reached a crescendo above the din of the audience. A waiter cleared their table, but still Adam did not speak.

'I should have died, Ayda,' he said, finally. 'I became separated from "A" Flight over Vimy when we engaged with about four red enemy Albatrosses. Terribly outnumbered, I knew I had precious little fuel left.' He paused, his eyes watering. 'Then I looked hard at the horizon, and, by the grace of God, I noticed them…' He stopped again, gulping some water.

'Go on, Adam, you know you can tell me anything, however frightful.'

'A group of six brown swerving machines; it was "A" Flight from a nearby squadron.'

The music quietened, the first chords of a solo violinist sweeping out from the orchestra.

'A most splendid formation it was — all Bristol Scouts. I could see the leader at the head of the diamond, and as the sun crept out, we were surrounded again by black crosses everywhere, all crashing down on our red and blue circles like an angry game of noughts and crosses. Except it was no game. No sooner had I started firing on one Hun plane, another appeared and dived on me. One, I remember, was blazoned with a black skull and crossbones, and then my Lewis gun jammed, so I started spinning and diving for all I was worth, trying to shake him off until I hid in a mass of cumulus clouds, but when I emerged, we were alone, and the plane that was chasing me was spinning towards the ground. Amazed, I looked around for my saviour — and then I saw him.'

'Who, Adam?'

'He was just a boy, Ayda. Not a burly man with broad shoulders but younger than me with a boy's face as white as the clouds around us. And something wasn't right.'

'How do you mean?'

'Waving one final time, the boy side-slipped down, disappearing into an enormous white cloud, and that's the last I saw of him.' Adam looked at her. 'You've heard about guardian angels, Ayda, haven't you?' He was looking straight at her. 'Well, that's what he was, I've no doubt. Sent by God himself. He saved my life that day, of that I am certain. It makes you appreciate life and it makes me not want to hang around and wait for things to come my way. Which is why I asked you here today.' Small beads of sweat were glistening on his forehead, his eyes fixing on hers, serious and dark.

Before she could even begin to think, the music relaxed to a softer tone, the violinist beginning a solo by Vaughan Williams, and Adam let out a long sigh as if the melody had released him from something. He took her hand in his, and shaking his head, he looked up as if seeing her for the first time.

'This isn't why I asked you here, Ayda, to talk of war, but I'll say just one last thing. We've a newcomer in our squadron, very similar to this boy, very much a lone wolf too.'

'Does your newcomer have a name?'

'Rick Randal. He's a bit older than the rest of us, but there's something about him. Some potential there, and you know he'd never let you down, would always be there for you. But he has something else: an inbuilt aggression, a real hatred of the Hun that goes far deeper than anything I've seen before.

'The men don't really like him. He started off on the wrong foot, he came across as a bit of a know-all, but it turns out he's a fine chap. He's already notched up twenty kills, M.C.'s in the bag too.'

Ayda had been surprised to be asked to dinner, but hadn't expected to be discussing schoolboy fighter pilots, guardian angels or squadron newcomers. She shifted in her chair.

'Look, Adam, it's been lovely seeing you again, and thanks awfully for dinner, but I've got an early start delivering my first F.E.8 to Gosport, so I best make tracks.' She had been watching the clock for a while now, wondering how best to make her excuses.

'Of course,' he said. 'That's it, by Jove! Ayda the pilot! I really have forgotten my manners. Well done! You must be completely chuffed with yourself, my girl — the first ever female dispatch pilot. What an honour! So, tell me, are you pleased?'

'I am, Adam, I really am,' she said, quickly settling back down again. 'And thank you for arranging everything at Farnborough.'

'Glad to be of service.'

'It's all been remarkably straightforward, though some people needed a bit of convincing that I was up to the job. Thankfully, that's all behind me now,' she said, picturing the assessor and her disabled aircraft.

'I should say so too! But if you're allowed to, can you tell me what you've been up to?'

She grinned. 'Well, initially I started delivering D.H.2s and recently I got to be relief mechanic at the Central after delivering there. I did that for a few days, though I'm not allowed to fly them over to France. I mean, I'm the only ferry pilot not given permission to deliver to St Omer — all because I'm a woman!'

Adam stared at her over the rim of his glass. 'Why would you want to go to France, Ayda, unless you really had to?'

'I've flown across the Channel on my own now, several times in fact.' Her green eyes widened further, challenging him.

'Look, Ayda, I of all people know exactly how capable you are because *I* recommended you in the first place. Haven't I always encouraged and believed in you? But there's a war out there, not some great adventure. People are getting killed. Leaving that aside, the planes coming out of Farnborough are often not properly configured. Some are pretty raw and have to be completely set up at St Omer before being channelled to the squadrons. Did I tell you about young Campbell last week?

Almost didn't make it, landed on the beach at Calais, having narrowly missed the cliffs at Dover.'

'Well, I'm sure I can swim as well as anyone else.'

Adam's jaw tightened. 'Look, I'm sorry to be so blunt, but France is no place for a woman at the moment, no place for a man either, but there we have it, we've got to see it through to the bitter end when both sides will have probably blown each other to bits. In any case, the arrangements I made for you were clear, Ayda. Very clear. You were to remain a civilian. You are not part of the R.F.C., because we do *not* have women pilots. And for very good reason.'

Grabbing her water in frustration, Ayda was reminded of the same words back at Farnborough. Why did everyone delight in making her feel small?

'I've seen some things … things which I still can't bring myself to talk about.'

Ayda looked up and saw the sadness in Adam's eyes.

'Ayda, I have three weeks leave, that is all, and I wanted to ask you something.' He gently squeezed her hand. 'You're one of my oldest friends and I find I have a great admiration for you. Your talents entrance me, in fact *you* entrance me. I feel very much alone in the world with the way my family are. Father's so busy now and mother's drinking is unbearable. I haven't heard from Granville, so I've no idea where he is now. And there's over sixty men at 39a, but none make me feel comfortable like you. What I'm trying to say is that I don't want to spend what time I have left on my own, so, will you do me the greatest honour of becoming my wife?'

Ayda stared at Adam in open-mouthed amazement. No longer able to hold his gaze, her eyes swept to the wall behind him.

'Please think about it, Ayda. There's no rush to make a decision, but I do like you awfully.'

Comfortable and *like you awfully*. She repeated the words in her head. Perhaps it was enough? This war had intensified everything, made things sharp, focussed. And she cared for him, too, had missed him. Perhaps that meant he was more than a friend. An awful thought occurred that maybe the next time he left it might be the last. As if on cue the music paused, waiting. They were still holding hands, and she cleared her throat, fingertips prickling with the same tension she usually felt before take-off.

'Yes, Adam. Yes, I will be your wife.'

'Good, I'm so pleased,' he said, patting her hand like it was a pet. 'That's settled then.'

'Well, yes, I suppose it is,' she said, looking at her fellow diners. Everyone was carrying on much as before, no one looking at them with envy or glee like something special had happened.

Now it was Adam who got ready to leave. 'Afraid I've got to push off back — boat early tomorrow, worse luck! Had to get special leave for this trip — told them Mother wasn't well; I didn't want to wait any longer to ask you.'

'So, no one at 39a knows you came home to propose?'

'Not a bean, Ayda,' he said, removing his hand and squaring his cap. 'Not really a reason for leave, eh? Still, they'll have to know some time, I suppose.'

'Yes, I suppose they will.' She looked away, feeling crestfallen. It had all sounded so important a moment ago — important to him, but now she wasn't so sure.

'Well, I shall tell my mother,' Ayda said. 'In fact, I've a few days off so that's what I think I'll do, go and see her.'

'Oh?' he said, inclining his head. 'Would you mind looking in on my mother as well? Perhaps you could tell her our news? I'll write to her but I'm not sure how quickly it will arrive.'

Ayda's stomach plummeted. He hadn't even told his mother? 'Oh,' she said. 'Yes, I suppose I can do that.'

A day later, Ayda arrived at her old cottage near Dunthorpe House. Rosina would be back early that afternoon or late evening, depending on when she had started that day, so, settling down, Ayda stretched out over her mother's thin bed frame. The journey from Farnborough had been long and tiring, and she felt in need of a rest.

A cockerel was singing loudly when she awoke, a scurrying sound coming from inside the room. Immediately her eyes sprang open to find her mother gathering items into a large wicker basket, unperturbed that someone was on her bed. Ayda sat up, then swung her legs across the bed.

'Mama!'

Rosina carried on with her tasks: stowing a fresh apron and stockings into her basket before moving towards the door. This was too much. Jumping up, Ayda got to the door first, barring her mother's exit.

'Mama,' she repeated, holding her arms out to her.

Rosina cocked her head to the side, eventually breaking into a smile. '*Ciao*, Graziella, *come stai*?'

Ayda frowned, taking her mother's rough and swollen hands in her own. Graziella was Rosina's sister. 'It's me, Mama, Ayda!'

Rosina's brown eyes blinked, a small smile brightening her pudgy face. '*Sì*, *sì*, Ayda.'

Ayda let out a breath, moving in closer but now, her mother's smile had evaporated, and she was fidgeting, tugging at her hair.

'*In ritardo per la scuola — vai, vai!*' Rosina moved towards her, shooing her out the door.

'Stop it, Mama. I am not late for school — there is no school anymore. Please!'

Her mother's agitation increased until Ayda was physically ejected into the garden. What could she do, and how could she pass on her news? More noise came from inside: furniture scraping along the floor, water splashing against the sink. The flowers in the garden shook their heads in the breeze as she stood mute with despair. Why hadn't her mother recognised her? Not wanting to go back inside, Ayda didn't feel much like going to the big house in pursuit of Lady Clarissa either.

No, Adam would have to do his own visiting.

Her appearance had somehow troubled her mother, she was anxious about something. And very unwell too.

Heading down the drive towards Aldenham village, Ayda considered her options. She would visit again when things were calmer, but who knew when that would be? Perhaps something planned might be better than just turning up out of the blue as she had done.

Her head had started aching, her fingertips prickling, and a sob caught in her throat as she marched herself down the winding drive. Her mother wasn't old, just forty years of age — what on earth was wrong with her?

CHAPTER 14

Adam had received a letter from his brother Granville: *Father drowned on the Hampshire.* Those five words turned his world upside down. Heart hammering, Adam fastened the entrance to his hut, and looked at the second envelope he had received. Postmarked Thurso, it was dated 4th June, 1916. It was from his father.

Dearest boy,

Enroute north by train for my latest adventure.

At least have been afforded my own compartment away from army bigwigs — thank goodness!

Weather abysmal: raindrops the size of dinner plates with Force 8 winds delaying departure at every station.

Heard from your brother who is seeing action with the Seaforths (letter enclosed), think you will be seeing the real stuff now with R.F.C.*!*

More news on return,

Father

P.S. No change with your mother

Adam quietly folded the letter into its envelope, glancing at the second one inside it, his brother's infantile scrawl recognisable anywhere.

Dear Father,

Greetings from 'la bonne' France, though I've yet to find anything 'bonne' about it. Anyway, couldn't miss the fun so got myself an outfit — anything I could find! Met up with some Scots in Canada and got this rather cushy number with the Seaforth Highlanders (that's the silly skirted variety with bagpipes etc.).

Seem to be doing all right. Enjoying bayonetting and teaching filthy Fritz a lesson or two and a few of the young'uns here as well. Got to break them somehow.

Yours

Granville

After a few days, Adam had managed to find out what had happened to his father. The HMS *Hampshire* was sailing full speed through the mine-infested western route of the Orkney Islands, when a gale forced the destroyer escort to return to Scapa Flow. The *Hampshire* was struck by a mine, and took just twenty minutes to sink. There had only been twelve survivors. His father, Lord Horatio Herbert Kitchener and countless others were now dead. Adam pictured the stormy scene: the sea jagged and swollen, the sky grey like charcoal. And his brother's face, laughing, jubilant: 'It's Lord Bound to you now.'

Flying back to Vert-Galant at ten thousand feet, his dawn-patrol completed, Adam looked over the side of his F.E.2b. His left-wing struts were badly frayed, some even broken and he swallowed hard, suddenly feeling faint, his mind re-reading Granville's wire: *Father drowned on the Hampshire.*

A pinprick of fire passed close to his head, then a tumult of bullets sprayed over the cockpit, and the Beardmore engine suddenly hiccupped. Adam jolted in his seat as if just awakened to find everything had gone silent save for a deafening whistling in the wires.

Grabbing his stick as the plane plummeted, the engine miraculously cut back in, the nose nudging upwards as the F.E.2b pulled itself up in the nick of time. What luck, he thought, his pulse recovering when his head swivelled round — something had caught his eye. Several thousand feet below, a tiny arc of yellow burst out across No Man's Land, reaching well inside the German lines. He checked his rear mirror. How strange — not anti-aircraft fire, or Archie as it was nicknamed, which he knew well, nor an explosion — he'd never seen anything like it.

Massaging his eyes with an oily glove, he re-checked his mirrors, put his nose down and dropped to three thousand feet. There he waited, circling, his heart missing a beat. Again, a tiny flash of red-orange unrolled like a carpet, disappearing in seconds. Intrigued, he dropped even lower, hovering at three hundred feet, wary of the ever-present Archie fire.

It was worth the wait. A massive arc of flames swept across the land straight into the German frontline, devouring everything in its path. But where was this fire-breathing dragon? Below, Adam could hear screams, terrified cries of burning Germans, and he vomited over the side of his plane, wondering if his father had screamed like that as his ship exploded, certain he would never forget these harrowing sounds of torture. Guns fired in the chaos, men were running in every direction, some half-dressed, some on fire.

Finally, he was noticed.

A volley of bullets shattered his glass visor, narrowly missing his head.

He'd seen enough. Kicking his rudder bar, he climbed through the sky, his head reeling, his heart bursting.

Back at Merville, Adam couldn't stop shaking. Having been in 39a Squadron for fifteen months now, he was by far the longest surviving member, avoiding both death and transfer on several occasions. The faces he'd started with: Hastings,

Devenport, Murphy and Beauly, his long-standing friends, were long gone. Only Rick remained.

Adam had finally discovered why Rick had such a violent hatred for the enemy. He had confided in Adam about his past.

'I was laying roads outside Athens in 1913,' Rick had told him. 'The following year, I arrived in Armenia to continue my work, but there were militants everywhere, many from just over the border. Anti-Christian, they were. As war broke out, I managed to escape being slung into a Turkish prison.' He ground his teeth. 'But not everyone was so lucky.'

'How the deuce did you end up working in such a far-off place?' Adam had asked.

'After finishing school at fourteen, I worked at a brewery with my uncle, but didn't much enjoy the work. Filthy and heavy, but at least it was outdoors, which I liked. Then my cousin got me a job as a bank clerk. I found the endless days of figures and ledgers tedious, and when I saw an advertisement for laying roads in the East, I knew it would get me outside again. I tendered my resignation and boarded the first ship across the Channel, making my way through to Greece where I remained for a year before crossing to Armenia in May 1914. That was the start of the Young Turk militant uprising.' Rick clenched his bony fingers into a fist. 'They used their power over us, we who had been laying their bloody roads day and night. One of my friends got thrown into a prison over the border in Turkey, and almost died from solitary confinement. He later escaped, but lost his mind shortly afterwards. So, shooting comes easy, my friend. I'll never let myself be put in that position again. No one is going to lock me up.'

The following day, Hastings had been shot through the head after encountering a lone Albatros over Béthune. After that, target practice intensified, Rick rising early each day, taking up an old B.E.2 unless on dawn patrol. Sweeping low over the airfield, he had a new target now: an old dartboard strapped to a piece of German fuselage. From heights of up to five hundred feet he aimed at the bullseye, over and over again. His shots became ever more accurate, and he'd easily overtaken Adam's score.

Adam had congratulated him, and suggested he take a break for a while, but Rick had declined. 'I need to know my aim will not fail me,' Rick said. 'Alone up there in the sky, it's us against them, you need every advantage, you should know that, my friend. My engine could misfire or my gun could jam, but I know I'll always win a duel. I'll shoot first and kill first, because I'm the best shot. That gives me power, and I like that, Bound, I really do. It's no game anymore.'

Adam couldn't help but admire Rick's honesty and dedication, knowing that 39a was a safer squadron for having him in it. Fifteen months at the front was an inordinately long time and Adam's own nerve was failing fast. What were the odds he could carry on and see the war out? One day soon it would be his turn to crash and burn…

CHAPTER 15

Ayda heard the postman long before the letter appeared.

1st July 1916

Dearest Ayda,

I hope you are well. We've been in quite a few scraps lately. In the last three days we've lost two machines, My nerves have remained steady though I've had a few scraps myself. Yesterday evening, my engine misfired at 16,000 feet and somehow, I got the bus down over our lines, hitting my arm in the process. Also managed to bring down an enemy bus with my single Lewis gun and 300 rounds — amazing when you consider his machine had two guns and 1000 rounds, though I confess I'm feeling like an assassin these days — not what I want. But too much talk of me, how are you, Ayda? Still taking your buses up and down the country, visiting all the little flying schools? Seems a jolly lark to me, so hope you're having fun!

I'm sorry, Ayda. You know I jest; you are doing a splendid job and I am very proud of you — the only fiancée I know with a ticket!

But have just remembered a deuce queer thing that I must tell you. Coming back from my dawn patrol today, I had just encountered a batch of Huns: four above and six below. Thought I was done for, but the cowards missed me, then flew east. As I dropped down thanking the Almighty, I noticed something odd: huge bursts of flames travelling over 100ft — Hun trenches burnt to a crisp. Felt thoroughly sick, but later remembered our 'friend' W. L. from the lecture. What do you think?

Ayda remembered it like yesterday: William Livens mobbed — Cameron Muir amongst them — how could she ever forget a meeting that she couldn't properly attend? Still, the chill of Livens' words made her feel Adam's horror.

No doubt you have heard the news of the sinking of the Hampshire? My father was with Kitchener until the end, and I now fear shockwaves will reverberate through the War Cabinet. I am, however, bearing up, but doubt his loss has sunk in properly.

On a more cheerful note, I will be on Home Establishment in October to do some important training so, if I'm still alive, and if you're not doing anything, perhaps we could get married then?

Kind regards

Adam

P.S. I have been awarded the D.S.O.

His letter was deeply unsettling. Seeing him mention their wedding in the same breath as the death of his father didn't sit right. Did Adam really love her? Or was he desperately seeking some sort of comfort by marrying her?

Later, when walking back to her lodgings, deep in thought, something caught her attention, a distant whiteness making her green eyes widen.

In a shop window, a floaty white dress shimmered against its dingy surroundings. Ignoring an omnibus lumbering past, Ayda crossed the road. Not suitable for evening or daywear, the dress was designed for one purpose only — to get married in, and with the mention of an October wedding playing on her mind, she moved in closer. The pearls sewn into the layers of silk shimmered in the sunlight, drawing her in, and the delicate diamonds entwined in the taffeta dazzled her through the glass window. The effect was stunning.

As she opened the door, a delightful warmth enveloped her body. Heady scents of vanilla and cinnamon wafted in the air and Ayda realised she was in a bakery. She asked why the dress was in the window.

'It's bad luck that dress is, miss,' a red-faced assistant explained. 'Made for our Else, it was, but she died of a broken heart on account of her fiancé dying at Loos. Then it passed to our niece, Beryl, but she don't want it neither, seeing as her man was gassed at Ypres. So, we thought we'd put it in the window and then when someone buys a wedding cake, they can take it too. But we ain't sold no wedding cakes since. Want it, do you, miss? Just order your cake, then you can 'ave it.' The flustered face looked hopeful, as Ayda hovered in the doorway.

Moments later, still with no date set, Ayda left carrying a large dress box, and a receipt for a wedding cake. The dress was beautiful, and she hoped it would bring her better luck than poor Else and Beryl.

She passed a newsstand. The early July newspapers were out, awash with optimism about the new Somme offensive: *The Sunday Pictorial* reporting: *The Big Advance: All goes well for England and France.*

Despite this encouraging report, Ayda felt even more apprehensive about Adam. Whenever she thought of this new Somme offensive, a familiar tingling in her extremities gave her a sense of foreboding. Shaking herself down, opening and closing her fingers, she gave herself a good talking to. No! She would not dwell on unpleasant thoughts.

Adam would come home, and they would have a beautiful autumn wedding. And maybe by then the war would be over…

CHAPTER 16

Early on 14th July, Adam set off on a special mission. Flying past Longueval in northern France, heading west near the village of Bazentin-le-Petit, he arrived at an area known as High Wood. High Wood sat up on a slope of slightly higher ground, offering a much-improved line of vision. As the wing of his Nieuport dipped to seven thousand feet, a faint, darkened outline of trees appeared ahead. A dry rasping cough shook his body as he descended through the cloud cover. The R.F.C. had thrown everything at these woods but still they remained impregnable.

That morning he was the eyes of the woods: flying low, checking through them over and over — the prelude to an attack.

At two thousand feet and still with a modicum of cloud cover, he dropped height. At one thousand feet he cut out his engine. The German Archie fire was sound asleep. Watching, listening, gliding his engineless Nieuport over High Wood, only the eerie whirring of the wind in his struts and ailerons sounded above the silent woods. Adam swallowed hard, listening, before turning on his ignition: the engine roared to life, lifting him back into cover.

Once safely out, Adam gave the signal. Infantry had been requested for the task but was held in reserve. As the ground of High Wood was deemed favourable for cavalry, regiments of the 20th Deccan Horse, an Indian cavalry unit, and the 7th Dragoon Guards, armed with lances gathered, then advanced. But twelve hours passed before they managed to cross the trenches, take up position, and finally attack. A few Germans surrendered, terrified by the cavalry in woodland.

But from the charge's optimistic start, the situation rapidly degenerated. Once the German's realised what was happening and started to retaliate, over a hundred men were killed along with one hundred and thirty horses. Barbed wire, mud and machine guns proved why cavalry charges were now seldom used in war.

In the mess, the assessment was brutal.

'When will the British Army grow up?' Rick Randal demanded, leaning hard against a billiard table. No one knew why a cavalry attack had been ordered. 'Horses are fine for pulling, but believing we can win this war on horseback is nothing short of insanity.'

Seated on a stool at the far end of the bar, Adam remained silent. He had been there at the start, checking for the enemy — and he'd seen no one. But by the evening everything had changed. The Germans had arrived. Why hadn't he been ordered to stay and assist from above? He could have helped. Nerves overwrought, he fidgeted uncomfortably.

'What do you say, Bound?' Rick turned to his friend. 'Out bright and early, chosen as the Signal man, you must have an opinion?'

'I've important letters to attend to.' Adam stood up, manoeuvring himself past the billiard table.

In the hut they shared, Rick found Adam sitting on his cot, a letter starting *Dearest Ayda*, in his hand.

'Sorry, old man. Didn't mean to upset you. A tad insensitive, but you know I don't mean it.'

'It's not just that, it's all about to get much worse.' Adam was close to tears. 'More ruddy flights: guiding the artillery, and two fighter squadrons as well. Who do they think we are? It's madness.'

'Well, anyone would think we're at war.'

'But they don't listen. Strange things are happening, Randal, I tell you. Take the other morning, admittedly I wasn't too bright and I'd just dodged a bit of Archie fire, but guess what I saw?'

'No idea. Lots of shell-holes?'

'Absolutely right, but something very odd too.' Adam sat back on his bed, knowing it was important Rick believed him. 'Moving ones. I kid you not, Randal, it was like they were alive. I went close several times, checking positions, and I swear, two or three of the holes moved.'

Rick walked over and sat down, his face serious now. 'I've seen something very similar too.'

Relief flooded Adam's face.

'Only last week, I reported it to HQ, and you know what they said? Don't be ridiculous, Captain Randal. Too much target practice and too many late nights. Have the R.A.M.C. look at your eyes.'

'I bet there's hundreds of Huns hiding beneath canvas,' Adam said, hanging his hands from his Sam Browne belt. 'That'll explain why they're always where we least expect them and popping up all over the place. Others have said the exact same thing but HQ say we're useless, that the clouds obstruct our vision or some such guff.'

'All they do is throw more guns and more men at them. But they're clever, those Germans, much cleverer than our stuffy old Generals with all their fun and games.' Rick pointed an accusatory finger in the air.

'Fun and games?'

'Surely, you've heard that, Bound?' Rick said, raising his eyebrows. 'The telephone calls between the Squadron C.O. and the artillery night and day — all with false positions and battle plans designed to confuse, but confuse whom, that's what I want to know? I can cope with four bombing patrols a day, dodging Archie fire, balloon strafing and the fighting — but not with this ridiculous trickery. Flying is straightforward, but this makes it a nonsense, and then I begin to doubt myself and think, am I where I'm meant to be? Am I at the right place, at the right time, or are my orders just to fool the Germans?'

'And what should we advise the men?' Adam said, warming to his friend's theme. 'It's all very well broadcasting the bombing of A or B so anyone could hear, then at the eleventh hour changing everything and rushing through the correct plans, or publicising that all movements are to be cancelled, then bombing anyway. But those Huns are good at separating fact from fiction, and before long someone's going to mess up. God knows, we're all so dog-tired.'

Rick swelled his chest out, looking pleased with himself. 'Rumour has it, or so I've heard, that roasted Hun's on the menu soon, grilling them with those flame projector thingamajigs, or some weapon of mass destruction: a Large Gallery Flame Projector, I believe.'

'Oh that! Sorry, old chap, seen it already. Flew down to three hundred feet over Mametz a few weeks back. Saw them running around all burning, and screaming. Awful…' Adam looked away at the memory. 'I met the inventor once… Seemed a nice chap.'

'Well, I never!' Rick's eyes widened. 'You lucky bugger, Bound. I'd have liked to have seen those rotters roast. Maybe next time, eh? Best let you finish your letter.'

Adam had forgotten the letter in his hand as he watched Rick leave. His friend's attitude always surprised him. Unlike him, he didn't hate the Germans with a passion. Putting the letter down, he pictured Ayda by the Old Sheds. Shutting his eyes, he looked inside, imagining the smells: hay, sweat, manure, seeing the horses; honest, trusting, toiling beasts, like those sentenced to death today…

A cold hand had hold of him these days. More newcomers came and went, but of his old friends, there was only Rick Randal… But had they even left? Perhaps their ghosts still inhabited the squadron, walking silently through the mess when no one was looking, taking up a plane or two. Adam shook himself hard. He'd heard that familiar thud-thud of an engine when he shouldn't have, and sometimes in the dead of night, he'd heard the clamour of a propeller rumbling in its housing when all the planes were tucked away under cover. He'd heard the creak of the old red dining chair too, inviting its next victim in, its leather flattening against a weight that just wasn't there.

Adam rubbed his eyes to stop the sickness rising. It was all ridiculous, he knew, but sometimes, just sometimes, he couldn't help his wandering thoughts.

Maybe there was something else at work, some inexplicable force from above, watching, deciding who should live and who shouldn't. He thought again of guardian angels. Maybe it was time to start believing in something not explained by science?

CHAPTER 17

Flinging the paper aside, Ayda's head rested on her hands. The fourteen-day Battle of Albert on the Somme, she had just discovered, was the bloodiest since war began, with around ninety thousand casualties, of which two thirds were on the first day. She knew the battle a few months back had been bad, but hadn't realised how bad. *Sixty thousand deaths in one day*, she read again, her gut wrenching. The towns of Montauban, Mametz, Fricourt, Contalmaison and La Boisselle buzzed round and round in her head — familiar, important names, knowing now they had been captured. Shaking her head, she picked up the newspaper again: field hospitals were still overflowing, stretcher bearers working flat out — a grim routine for a grim life.

Ayda had settled into a routine, delivering planes from Farnborough to the Central Flying School. Each morning by ten o'clock, air speed, wind direction and cloud cover would be checked, so she could determine the feasibility of flying the sixty-mile journey to Upavon.

Ayda put the paper away and made her way to work. The day was turning out to be fine, with soft pillowy clouds. When she arrived, she found her flying contraption for the day was a rounded missile-shaped version of an Airco pusher, and after reaching a nippy 100 mph with good visibility all round, she relaxed into her seat.

Up and up the plane went: one thousand feet — two thousand feet — three thousand feet and beyond.

Easing the stick more sharply made it pitch up and down precariously like a see-saw.

At five thousand feet, Ayda recorded the time: a respectable twelve minutes, though the need for left rudder had made it a slightly tiresome climb. Overall, stability and roll were fair to good.

Assessment complete, the hilly, Wiltshire airfield of the Central came into view with its weatherboard huts straddled between north and south aerodromes like miniature treehouses.

An unpleasant thought entered her head. Why was *she* seeing new planes before the men fighting? Was this right? Her job was to deliver planes — not assess them. The men fighting had to put up with whatever was sent their way and they'd been sent some truly dire machines in the past.

Approaching the Central, the crosswinds buffeted and she was reminded how many pilots bemoaned that the aerodrome was open to every wind, but today challenging landing conditions weren't her only worry. As the green peaks of the north aerodrome sprung into view, Ayda saw a group of pilots waiting for her. Taking off her helmet and goggles and unwrapping her scarves after she landed, releasing her long hair, their shocked faces made her think that if a dog had landed the plane rather than a woman, they would be happier. She gave them a little wave and they retreated.

The pilots here at the Central considered themselves elite, often sent for betterment to sit practical and written examinations. Many looked haughtily at all delivery pilots, and Ayda knew even her male counterparts felt inferior. She too dreamed of attending lectures, studying for examinations, but that furtherment was never offered.

Later that day, at Farnborough, her unease returned. Some squadrons had received the new single-seat French Nieuport 17 with its powerful Le Rhône rotary engine. 39a Squadron had a few, but to her horror, had been sent more F.E.8s, termed 'Fighter Experimentals', probably the last plane she would ever consider a fighter. F.E.8s not only looked ridiculous but were cumbersome brutes to fly and tricky to recover from in a spin. Again, her heart lurched, but what could she do? How could anyone fly a bulky beast like an F.E.8, scan for the enemy, aim, shoot and reload, all at the same time? It wasn't surprising that so many British pilots lost control and descended into a deadly spin.

Standing by a hangar, signing off her delivery, conversation then took a welcome turn, and Ayda's ears pricked up. Talk was of the long-awaited Scout Experimental or S.E.5 with its three prototypes due next month. The brainchild of Farnborough's best designers, Henry Folland, John Kenworthy and Major Frank Goodden, Ayda knew that if they couldn't stop the 'Fokker Scourge', then nobody could. Not quite believing her ears, she prayed that this new S.E. was the answer, and that she would be the first dispatch pilot to fly it.

A few weeks later, she wrote to Adam.

7th November 1916

Dearest Adam,

Hoping you are safe and well. I wasn't surprised your October leave was cancelled. We hear of another big push all the time, and I've never delivered so many planes. Am still enjoying the work immensely though. Please let me know if you can get leave for Christmastime. We can plan for then as I would like the wedding in London or Farnborough — not at home — I will explain why. I have also obtained a suitable dress; however, I do not have good news following your suggestion I visit home, much has changed there, and I hardly know where to begin.

Radlett village is like a ghost town with only Mrs Bellson occasionally at the school, which remains closed. A handful of girls hang around, but no boys. No one can be spared for education it seems, and Cameron Muir has a post at the War Office.

My old house is boarded up along with all the cottages in the terrace. Walking to Dunthorpe House, I was unable to enter through the main entrance, so was met at the west gate by Baxter. Your home, Adam, has been requisitioned by the War Office, and is now a hospital and convalescent home. The front lawn was decked out with wheelchairs, and just north of the main gate is a large assessment marquee like a dressing station. The wounded are particularly disfigured as the hospital specialises in burns and facial injuries; I'm sorry to say there were several aviators there too. On finding Baxter again, I was told Lord Bound had recently visited. Not your father, but your brother, Granville, who is very much alive with a commission in the Seaforth Highlanders, and at present stationed at Harbonnières. Wonders never cease — where will he appear next?

Baxter, as with all good butlers, never gives anything away but hesitated when asked if I could see my mother and Lady Bound. Finally, I was taken to the west wing where I found both our mothers. Rosina, I don't think, recognised me. Your mother was propped up in bed with her head slumping over, her hair although red in parts, was mainly grey. Her skin looked awful; paper thin, sallow, and very yellow. I'm sorry to be so detailed, but felt you should know, but when my mother looked right through me, I fled the room. Later, Baxter found me, told me she had worsened in the last six weeks, now only speaking of her childhood and only in Italian. I left immediately without looking in at the Old Sheds, not even checking on your dear Blackburn. Sorry! But I know I won't ever go back again, and, should you insist on us marrying there, then I will have to refuse you. It is too distressing.

Please can we agree on either Farnborough or London?

Yours most sincerely,

Ayda

P.S. I must thank you for the beautiful gold sweetheart brooch. I can now pin the letters R.F.C. *to my flying jacket despite only being a civilian pilot!*

CHAPTER 18

Three days before Christmas, Adam arrived at Hainault Farm in Essex, with a temporary posting as Flight Commander at 390 Squadron. Surveying the flat countryside, he soon spotted a makeshift aerodrome with several canvas huts and a single metal hangar with a tractor in the foreground. Gravel crunching underfoot soon announced the arrival of a large man. Standing well over six feet tall, with a bushy head of hair and a circular disk for a face, he smiled down extending a beefy hand.

'Good morning, guvnor. Corporal Williams at your service.' The voice was deep, jovial. 'We've been expecting you, Captain Bound. Here for a spot of the old Zepp strafing?'

'Something like that, Corporal...'

'Fancy doing a Leefe Robinson, do we?' Williams asked, not waiting for an answer. 'Of course, you do. I was there, you know — stationed at Suttons Farm down the road when he took off in one of the old B.E.2 buses. First of our boys to shoot down a German airship! Been busy since. Seen nothing like it meself. We've got Strutters now. Ever flown one, sir?' The big man paused, allowing Adam time to reply, and, as if on cue, a Sopwith Strutter was wheeled out.

'No, I can't say I have, Corporal, only B.E.2's and very recently Nieuport 17's.' Adam glanced nervously at the Strutter.

'I'll tell you a secret if you keep mum about it.' Williams crept closer, checking they wouldn't be overheard. 'We've got the Big Pup here as well, we have — flown in yesterday — en route to Brooklands ready for Christmas. All shiny and the only one too, though word's out that we'll all be getting them next year.'

'Big Pup?'

'Sopwith Camel, guvnor. Couldn't believe me eyes when it landed — it were a woman flying it! Delivered by a woman.' Williams shook his large head. 'Whatever next, I says to meself? And a very fine looking one too — excellent mechanic by all accounts. Just flew in, she did, could have landed it on a halfpenny, I'd say. Amazing!'

Adam suddenly felt very proud — Ayda must have done well.

Williams didn't notice him smiling and continued. 'Naturally, your Camel here's a different beast, the latest single-seater scout with a 110hp Le Clerget engine and not one, but two Vickers guns. Maybe you're to fly the Strutter, sir? Anyways, I didn't finish telling you about Captain Robinson. The 2nd of September it was. He took off before midnight with Lieutenant Sowerby and not a full tank of petrol neither. And just after the a.m. he saw the bastards flying over Woolwich unloading their bombs, climbing higher and higher, the tracers not touching them neither.'

Adam politely listened to the now famous story, unsure which plane he would be flying — the Strutter, or like Leefe Robinson, the B.E.2c, though he was desperate to try the Camel that Ayda had just flown in, but still the large man talked on.

'He let them have it, he did. It were a Schütte-Lanz SL 11, and he emptied not one, but two drums into it — still it went on flying until Captain Robinson made another attack from astern, emptying his final drum into the twin rudders. And then the Zepp went all red like, and whoosh…' Williams spluttered through his teeth, expanding his spade-like hands.

'Whoosh I says, then it burst into flames and like a burning fireball it fell from the sky. And Robinson got back to Suttons Farm just before three in the morning — a right proper hero he was, and we carried him shoulder high in the aerodrome. But do you know what?' The corporal wheezed, taking a longer breath. 'After all that fun and frivolity, and after three and a half hours flying, he went straight to his desk and wrote his report! That's when we decided we'd call it Zepp Sunday.'

Adam decided to speak, wondering how many people Williams had entertained with his tale. 'Yes, Corporal, I read about Robinson's V.C. in October. Lord Northcliffe's *Daily Mail* gave a very detailed account. Most deserved. I only hope I don't disgrace myself as I've never done any night flying.'

Williams lowered his moon-like face, now curious. 'If you don't mind me asking, sir, how comes you're here just before Christmas? Not much time to bag a Zepp! October's the time. We was out flying every night then, them swarming all over London. This month and last, they've gone quiet. Getting ready for Christmas they are, because them Huns like their Christmases, don't they, guvnor?'

'Indeed, they do,' Adam agreed, 'and perhaps they might allow me mine so I can get married. You see, I'm getting wed on New Year's Eve. You met my fiancée yesterday, Corporal — Ayda Gulzar — the Camel pilot.' He had waited for the moment, and the corporal's face didn't disappoint.

Folding his oversized arms, Williams beamed down. 'Well, I never. That's just splendid, sir. Absolutely splendid! Very much in love, are we, guvnor?'

'I suppose I am, Corporal — whatever love is. Anyway, she's a marvellous girl.'

A dreamy look settled over the corporal's large features. 'If you don't mind me saying, sir, there should be no *suppose* about it. Now take my Bertha and me. She's my true l—'

'Yes, well, thank you, Corporal Williams,' Adam cut him short. 'Some other time, perhaps? It's been a long day, and we haven't yet established which plane I'm flying. I'd also like to be shown my quarters if you don't mind?'

Later, relaxing in an armchair, Adam wondered why the corporal had irritated him so, knowing that he was about to say: *true love.* But Ayda was a fine girl — with a better mathematical brain than him — the only girl he knew with an Aero Club ticket. She was dependable, pretty, and a good friend. Stretching his legs across the bedframe, he sank into the mattress — yes, it felt good to be on home soil.

Hours later, dozing on and off, he awoke with a start, thinking of the wedding, and of Ayda. Back at 39a Squadron, his announcement had produced much backslapping, whoops, and drinks all-round. Almost everyone was pleased. Only Rick Randal looked bemused.

What was he thinking — taking someone in his arms — pretending love with them just because the notion of loneliness horrified him? He'd clung to Ayda who cared about him thinking it would suffice, but marrying for life scared him — and worst of all, in front of an altar. Fortunately, they'd invited no one — wartime weddings didn't require guests. Thinking of Corporal Williams, Adam knew he didn't know what *true love* meant, he'd never known love at home, doubted he was even capable of it. And what he was about to do made him feel sick to the core, but he knew his duty. He wouldn't let Ayda down. Certainly not at the altar.

Through the skyline window, the beginnings of a night sky crept in along with the silvery beams of moonlight. He felt a familiar aching… When had he last spent a night alone under the stars with his maps, pinpointing constellations, nebulae or just greeting the brightness of Sirius or Jupiter? The stars and planets were always there watching, guiding as he tore across the sky like a lunatic in search of the enemy. They never let him down. And when had he last taken out his beloved reflector?

Per ardua ad astra, through adversity to the stars, was the Royal Flying Corps' motto and a very fitting one too.

Ayda accepted his passion for the stars, asking no questions, and he wished he could feel the same longing for her. Wiping away a tear, he dozed again before the familiar thud-thudding of engines roused him, and he remembered where he was.

'Patrol at ten, guvnor,' came a deep voice. 'Mechanics firing up your Strutter now, sir.' A mug of steaming tea sat beside him, a large shadow retreating into the background.

Adam had never flown at night. Not many pilots had, and his Strutter, like most planes, had no lights, but two things comforted him. First, the full moon afforded considerable light, as did two large searchlights: one to the north, and one to the south of the capital. And second, several lines of red and golden flares lit the aerodrome. These were ingeniously made from petrol tins cut at the top, stuffed with cotton waste then drenched in liquid paraffin.

Mentally checking engine revs, speed and oil pressure, feeling for his compass, a euphoria, long forgotten, overwhelmed him, reminding him of the early days of learning to fly by feel or instinct. And, for the first time ever, he got his wish — flying beneath the night sky. Between the moonlight and the searchlights, he was surprised at how much he could see and the detail too. Easily tracing railway tracks by metal shimmering in the night, a wavy pattern weaved over the land so that when a train passed, it snaked like liquid gold along its lines. And everything reflected the soft beautiful moonlight — even the Thames rippled and glistened as it divided London's north and south, its boats delicately silhouetting against the sea. Tiles on rooftops glimmered like thousands of tiny mirrors, but nothing compared to the night sky. Jupiter shone brightly, and the constellation of Cassiopeia with its distinctive W shape, could easily be seen. He also spotted Mars skulking low to the right of Venus. After two hours, he was content that his allotted Hun spotting had passed without incident, but he was sad to leave the sky.

It was time to land. The Strutter, he discovered, was one of the lightest planes to fly. Gently feeling his way, watching for the flare lines, he could position his rudder near the first line, the rotary engine groaning as he opened it up for an instant, then spluttering as he eased it off. Flicking it back on again for the odd burst, Adam glided downwards until, holding both his breath and the stick, he felt the wheels and tail touch down.

Filling in his flight report after midnight, Adam reflected on the most perfect flying he'd ever done — all in darkness and without seeing a single enemy plane. Tonight, he'd managed to combine flying with his first love, the stars, and was grateful to Ayda, for had they not been marrying, he'd never have put in for Home Defence, never have discovered the joys of night flying.

The elation made him restless, and sleep was late in coming. Again, the stars worked their magic so that when he awoke, he looked forward to the following week — and to his wedding.

CHAPTER 19

The grey spires of St Pancras rose above the day's mist, blending effortlessly with the capital's gloom. Scenes of chaos unfolded as platforms heaved with a mass of moving khaki, bags, people — all dragging up and down staircases.

'Goodbye, luv,' a soldier said, holding onto his sweetheart.

Alighting from the 14:06 from Essex, Ayda narrowly avoided the couple: a brown-coated female in a flowery hat, clinging to her soldier love.

'Promise you'll write?'

'Course I will, luv, you know I will.' The soldier fiddled with his Sam Browne.

'Say it won't go on much longer?'

Turning away, he eyed the station clock with despair, a whistle sounding above a funnel's hissing. Moving back, the soldier pulled the woman closer, kissing her passionately. He kissed away the tears streaming down her face before finally heaving his kit bag, and boarding the train.

Ayda stood, transfixed, aware she was staring.

The woman sprinted to an opened window, the train pulling away — metal on metal screeching from its tracks.

'Look after yourself, luv,' the soldier said, hanging from the window.

Flowery hat sliding to the ground, the woman shook with emotion, the train vanishing from view as Ayda bent down to pick it up.

'Goodbye my love,' the woman whispered, blowing a kiss into the steam.

The hat felt warm against her fingers despite the December cold, but when Ayda stood up, the woman had vanished too. Watching them for almost ten minutes, she doubted they'd even noticed her, and was sad for their pain, their separation — but not for their love. She pictured her departures from Adam: a quick handshake, a wave, and most recently holding hands tightly, feeling his warmth and not wanting to let it go.

Setting off from St Pancras, weighed down by the heavy wedding dress in her suitcase, she recalled the woman's last words, not even catching their names — they had only ever said *love.* She thought of why she was in London — her wedding — her fiancé — her dearest, oldest friend. But never *my love.*

The Cavendish, a bright but forgettable red-bricked hotel was situated at 28 Bruton Street in Mayfair, convenient for the R.F.C. Club where Adam was staying. The small bauble fir tree in reception reminded her it was the season of goodwill, and Ayda wondered if this extended to the Germans. Number 13 Bruton Street was the site of the new R.F.C. Club and Adam had been invited to its opening and inauguration in the New Year by the founder, Lieutenant Colonel Bersey.

It was almost 1917. And still they were at war.

Alone in her hotel room, her thoughts turned to the couple at the station from earlier. Placing a hand over her heart, Ayda concentrated. Nothing! She thought of Velma and Mabel, the women she had typed with, but unlike them, she felt no yearning, nor fluttering of heartstrings. Only despair. She'd allowed her judgement to be skewed because of the war and the gratitude she felt towards Adam for her work, believing she owed him her hand. Obviously, he harboured deep romantic feelings else he never would have proposed, it was a just pity she couldn't reciprocate them. But she would do her duty. A man's duty involved fighting for King and Country, sometimes even to the death. But men, she decided, were strange beings, and even the unruliest aircraft was infinitely more straightforward.

She thought about her wedding dress, and she remembered the sad tale of poor Else and Beryl. No! It *would* bring her luck… Whatever she did, she knew she cared for Adam, was grateful to him, her love of flying was discovered through him, so love would be too. It was only this dreadful war making everyone forge ahead without proper thought — that was no one's fault, certainly not theirs.

Adam joined Ayda for dinner at the Cavendish Hotel with one or two others in his regiment. Talk was of the Zeppelin attacks and Leefe Robinson's Victoria Cross, the first ever awarded to a member of the R.F.C. Then it moved to 2nd Lieutenant Tempest, who had also downed a Zeppelin in a field near Potters Bar killing its entire crew. He'd been awarded the D.S.O. and although impressed, Ayda expressed the view that they were only doing their jobs, that many of the raids abroad were just as hazardous, and never got the same recognition. The other guests stared at her as if she were mad. They didn't agree, and Ayda prayed for a change in conversation.

That night, Ayda once more found herself alone in her hotel room — her wedding hotel, she thought, trying to get excited. But with no guests, and feeling very alone, she dearly wished she could talk to someone.

On 31st December 1916, at a small chapel in the shadow of the magnificent St George's Church in Hanover Square, she shimmered in her white taffeta and lace dress, its layers of silk and pearls sparkling in the candlelight. In a ceremony with no family, no friends and perhaps no love, Ayda Gulzar married the Honourable Adam Bound.

PART 3

CHAPTER 20

April 1917

The statistics made grim reading. Ayda sighed, moving the paper away, but then she went back to it, hoping everything had changed. It hadn't. Two hundred and forty-five aircraft lost, two hundred and eleven aircrew killed or missing with one hundred and eight taken as prisoners. By comparison, the German Air Services had lost just sixty-six aircraft… It was the R.F.C.'s worst month to date, which the papers had dubbed 'Bloody April'. Feeling languid and tearful, she wondered why she bothered reading the newspapers, especially before setting off on a mission. There never seemed to be any good news and it always made her feel worse. Her head throbbed and her stomach churned, but wild horses wouldn't deter her from flying, for she was to pilot one of the first S.E.5a's to Dover, ready for dispatch to France.

When she reached the airfield, Ayda began to feel unwell. Nausea forced her to miss the first convoy, and as she prepared to set off with the second, she took a moment to appraise the new machine, hoping it would distract her from how she was feeling. She admired the wooden box-like structure covered in canvas. The S.E.5 didn't appear out of the ordinary at first glance, but looks were often deceptive for it had been designed with stability and handling in mind. Behind and under the upper wing, the pilot could sit in the centre with unobstructed views. For the men across the Channel, it was the interrupter gear that was important: a Vickers gun firing through a two-blade propeller via a Constantinesco interrupter gear. At long last, here was a machine that fired in the direction it flew with no interruption to the pilot, and she was thrilled to be sending it on its way.

Once she was up in the air and en route to Dover, Ayda could hear the guns above the wind and engine noise, and was glad that a real fighter would finally be crossing the Channel. But for many, she knew, the S.E.5 was still a distant dream. 'All squadrons should have them!' she shouted into the wind.

As her frustration boiled over, she was disturbed by another wave of nausea, and after a hasty landing, found herself vomiting into a rusty oil drum. Two mechanics chuckled to themselves as they watched her.

'First, they want the vote, now they think they can fly,' one of them said, smirking. 'You mark my words; she'll be after your job next.'

The second man looked unconvinced, as she retched. 'Nah,' he said, 'think you're worrying over nothing. Looks like a bleeding mess to me. Too much for 'em. Body's just not built for it, I says.'

'Perhaps you're right,' the first man agreed, leaving Ayda clinging to her oil drum.

It didn't take long for Ayda to confirm she was pregnant. She had suspected it as soon as the vomiting started. She was never travel sick, no matter how rough her flying conditions and she knew from the gossip she heard during her typing job that nausea was a common early sign you were with child.

After the initial shock, she tried to forget about it and immerse herself in her new role as owner of Audley House, the town house that had been bequeathed to Adam once they were married. There was much there to distract her. Lining the west side of Regent's Park, surrounded by ash, beech and birch trees, Audley House was an elegant Georgian property within a group of white stucco terraces. It came with twenty-five rooms, an enviable sized garden, and a full complement of staff. It had been strange moving in without Adam. He had barely had time to spend the night with her after their wedding before flying back to the front, but he had given her the address and written to notify the staff of her arrival. Ayda was struggling to get used to such a lavish lifestyle. Her life with her mother had always been a simple one, and though she was intelligent and educated, she had no one to guide her on how to run a household.

She could feel the servants judging her and she had no one to confide in about her pregnancy. Things were becoming difficult: her emotions were all over the place; one minute she was so elated by the thought of a future with Adam and their unborn child that tears fell freely, the next, she felt numb and cold when she remembered how alone she was.

She knew she must write to her husband, but what should she say? They had never discussed the issue of children. She didn't know if Adam would be pleased or horrified by the news. But she needed his support. Putting pen to paper at last, Ayda prayed the battles around Arras wouldn't prevent her letter getting through to him.

CHAPTER 21

'Clever girl,' Adam whispered, closing the envelope. His flying clothes lay draped across his cot bed, ready, his fur-lined boots polished for the freezing temperatures of fifteen thousand feet. He read the letter again, still only remembering three words: *I am pregnant.*

He looked again at his boots, his clothes. They looked as they normally did, and he supposed things would just carry on. Except that now things were anything but normal. He'd been given the most amazing news. Re-reading Ayda's letter a third time, he noticed the date: 30th April 1917. Three months ago. Why had it taken so long to reach him? He needed to respond quickly. She must be wondering why he had not yet replied.

The roar of a newly fired Le Rhône engine brought him back to his surroundings: outside, a group of Nieuport 17s was taxiing around the airfield. Repeating those three words as he dressed for his patrol, he smiled again. His marriage may have had a shaky start, but, like flying, it was filled with surprises and it would all be all right now. Outside, the sky was a perfect blue. A good omen, he thought. Should he tell the men his news? No, he decided. He'd tell it to the sky first.

Tiny puffs of clouds like white meringues swirled lazily in the breeze, playing a game of hide and seek with the sun's rays, as Adam made his ascent. Things were going right, at last, and he might just come through this nightmare after all. Since the awful days of Bloody April, the R.F.C. had done an about-turn. Fighting machines were arriving in numbers at St Omer: mostly S.E.5a's and Sopwith Camels. Ayda would be in her element. Her work made him immensely proud, and he knew she would be sorely missed. She was one of the most capable dispatch pilots available. Still, it couldn't be helped. She had a new purpose now.

Smiling for the umpteenth time that day as their patrol passed over Douai, he waggled his wings at the two new recruits, Phipps and Harker, and carefully dodged some Archie fire. Today, the sky was the bluest he'd ever seen, and unaccountably deserted.

Ayda's letter had come at just the right time, for Adam had been dealing with much more unwelcome news. Meeting up with Cyril Crowe, 56 Squadron's C.O., the day before, he found out that Crowe had been the last person to see the now famous ace Albert Ball alive. Reluctant to give up his trusty Nieuport 17 for a new S.E.5a, Ball had emerged from a dark storm cloud in the new plane, confused, and collided with Lothar von Richthofen of Jasta 11. The German had survived. Understandably, the R.F.C. were in deep shock, still mourning their twenty-year-old ace. There had been no guardian angel for him.

Hearing a slight hissing noise, Adam glanced down at his oil pressure gauge. The pressure was dropping fast. Damn! It never paid to let up even for a few seconds. Looking to his right, he realised he had inadvertently led his patrol into a massive barrage of Archie fire coming from Sallaumines. A stream of bullets peppered the sky as he expertly raised his nose, signalling to his two protégés to head for home. Aware the sibilating sound had increased, Adam checked his instruments, hoping he too could limp home.

And then he saw them.

Four dark dots, right out in front.

Soon the hissing spray was unbearable, and his Nieuport shuddered as it lost height.

Still they headed towards him, getting larger by the minute.

And ruining *his* sky. His perfect azure-blue sky. And his perfect day.

He could forgive them anything — except that.

Adam shook his elevator stick with rage, noticing it shook back, coated in a thick layer of oil. Soon his gloves were coated too, and his goggles dripped with the stuff. The Nieuport bent its nose downwards.

But he really didn't want to leave this sky — not yet. Nor did he want to leave his wife, so wonderful, so clever. And yes, he truly believed he loved her after all. He understood it all now … stupid to have doubted it before … he had it all straightened out in his mind. And there was this new life now…

His Nieuport shook as its struts whined and its wings vibrated dangerously. The dark dots were huge blobs now. Grubby, angry blobs blocking out everything. A total abomination! One even had the audacity to be coming straight at him. And fast!

What a cheek! How could he see anything now?

Closer it came. Faster still.

He could see the German's white teeth through his layer of black. See his mouth contort into a sickening grin against the grime of his face, and the black of his goggles. His teeth shone against the muck and dirt polluting *his* sky.

The damned blighter — who did he think he was?

A new screeching noise sounded from Adam's wires, deafening him, and still the spray of oil and black kept coming. The viscous, cloying muck plugged his nostrils, made him gasp, made him choke. The fumes were strong, sickening, pungent, heady. His boots felt thick, his feet plastered. And his head swivelled round and round. The beautiful blue had vanished. He could barely see through the black fug.

Still, he knew it was coming. Incandescent with rage, Captain Adam Bound shook his fist, and shouted, 'This is my sky and I am not leaving it. So, get out!'

An earthshattering splintering followed — then a dull thud as the Nieuport 17 and Albatros D.III collided in the sky. A massive ball of flames fanned over both planes before consuming them.

CHAPTER 22

We regret to inform you Captain Adam Bound is missing in action since 29th July 1917.

A young post boy plopped the cable into Ayda's lap then pedalled away, his whistling ringing in her ears as she sank to the ground, covering her face with muddied hands.

In the walled garden, a garden full of life, Ayda wondered how she could face her life alone. With the baby due in only a few weeks, she had been trying to look forward to it, but now everything had changed — her new life vanishing on the say so of a sentence. More than that, another good, innocent man had vanished for no other reason than war.

Raw with emotion, Ayda wasn't sure who she was crying for: Adam, herself, their baby, or the poor broken world left behind. The rough ground was uncomfortable but she didn't care, guilt had made her more uncomfortable — after all, she'd never even told him she loved him. Adam was the kindest person, her best friend, and yet she had doubted his feelings for her. His love. And her own. His actions should have given her a clue — and now it was too late.

The following morning, cable in hand, the tiled foyer of the new R.F.C. Club stood before Ayda. Ayda rang the bell and a small white-haired porter appeared, barring her entrance into the club, reminding her that women were not permitted. He checked, but they had no further news of Adam and no correspondence in his pigeonhole. Ayda kept trying for a further week until the porter grew exasperated.

'Look, madam,' he glanced at her swollen belly, 'you're in no fit condition to be coming down here every day crying and fretting. We have Captain Bound's address in London, and we'll contact you there if there's any news.'

'But, see here,' she said, waving her cable. 'It says *missing* in action, not *killed*. There is a difference.'

The porter looked at her kindly. 'Only that no body's been found yet. But we know where to find you, madam, should we have any news.'

What else could she say? She crept away before she was forced to leave.

In her blue papered bedchamber, on the last day of August 1917, the pains started. Ayda closed her eyes, part of her hoping death would take her. The pains were relentless; a knife twisting, digging deeper and deeper inside. In between screams, she would doze off, then it would start over and over again throughout the night. She hadn't wanted fuss, nor to go to hospital, and now, she felt she didn't want the baby either.

Just before noon on the 1st September 1917, she gave birth to a baby girl. Too exhausted even to look, the tiny bundle rolled off her body, caught at the last minute by her maid Bintie as Ayda drifted into a fitful sleep.

Hours later a faint cry awakened her. The baby, she thought, not particularly interested. Someone brought it to her and a rounded little cherub face with the darkest eyes she had ever seen, stared back. But there were other things she noticed — strange things, skin-like protuberances over her face, and she turned away in shock. A feeble cry made her look again, this time at the infant's rose petal lips which were a dusky-blue colour, her little fists clenched together as she gulped and struggled to breathe.

Not believing this was happening, Ayda sat bolt upright, eyes blazing. 'She doesn't look right. My baby's sick. We have to do something!' Tears bubbled to the surface.

'There, there, Miss, just a good feed is all baby needs,' Bintie soothed. 'And mother's milk is best for 'em, I should know, I've raised eight. Whatever would Master Adam say with you fretting so?'

As if he could say anything, Ayda thought, which brought on more tears. She was sore, tired and the baby had serious problems which she didn't know how to solve.

'There, there, Miss. Baby blues, that's what they call it. I had it bad with me last four, I did.'

'Thank you,' Ayda croaked, 'you're probably right.'

After a few weak cries, the baby's fists clenched then unclenched as she tried feeding, before stopping, exhausted, her dark eyes looking up at Ayda as if to apologise, her chest barely rising.

Later, muffled noises from the servants were audible from outside the room. Whispers of *not right*, *not normal* rang in Ayda's ears when they thought she was resting. Looking at the baby's chest, she noticed the left side was enlarged, that the dusky-blue colour had now spread over her mouth, and that her daughter's legs lay strangely flat against the crib like a small frog. Ayda sat on her bed assessing her like a scientific problem. Her instincts had been right.

'Help me dress, please, Bintie, I'm taking Katia to hospital and will require a cab immediately.' As soon as the baby's name left her mouth, Ayda knew it was right. Katia was her mother's middle name.

'Katia? The baby? Oh no, Miss,' Bintie said. 'You'll catch a death of a cold if you go out now. London can be ever so chilly in September, if you please.'

'Thank you, Bintie. But I must go to Bloomsbury. Now!'

Katia was wrapped and swaddled in the warmest shawl Ayda could find, and they soon arrived at the footsteps of the Hospital for Sick Children at number 49 Great Ormond Street.

The imposing red-brick building with its twin turreted towers looked oddly out of place in the staid surroundings of Bloomsbury, like a shining monument at the centre of a coal-choked city.

Hours later, a quietly spoken nurse with a Scottish accent ushered Ayda into a small room by a magnificent wooden staircase. The room was marked Parents' Room, and inside its spartan interior, Ayda crumpled onto a bench: a widow, a solitary parent preparing for more angst and heartbreak. None of this seemed right. She had achieved impossible things in her life, could solve problems others could only dream of, yet simple things alluded her: a family, holding her husband and baby.

'Mrs Bound,' the nurse said, 'there is no easy way to say this, but your daughter is very poorly.' She spoke to soothe, and might have succeeded if not for what she was saying. 'There are a number of problems, not least her hips, which are dislocated and will need splinting. Mr John Wycliffe Peck has pioneered a number of orthopaedic splints for children which are fireproof, and he is arranging this for Katia.'

The nurse paused a moment, but Ayda felt too exhausted to respond.

The nurse continued. 'Her facial skintags can be removed by tourniquet at a later date.' Then she hesitated. 'Mrs Bound, your wee one has cyanosis. You may have noticed a blue tinge to her skin? It is not a diagnosis in itself but a symptom of a serious, underlying problem. You see, she has heart problems. We would like to open her chest to see if we can do anything. I must stress, we are one of the few hospitals with the new X-ray machines and…' A longer pause ensued. 'She is almost certain to die within days if we do nothing. She may, however, have a chance if we do.'

The room started spinning. Ayda felt herself detach and look down at somebody who resembled her. She watched this person sign a consent form, be pointed towards a park and told to walk in the sunshine while she waited. She had wanted to show her baby the sun, the blue sky, her daddy's beloved stars, dress her in beautiful clothes. Katia was just over a day old, and Ayda knew she had never loved anyone or anything as much in her life.

'Please go now, Mrs Bound. Come back here at noon and we will discuss Katia's aftercare.'

Ayda slipped away, doing as she was told, dread and despair accompanying.

The hours slipped by, the sun barely warming her cold hands. At the appointed time, she arrived back at the hospital, feeling sick. Several people had gathered, and she looked for the Scottish nurse amongst them. In the tiled foyer, a few stony-eyed doctors avoided her eye. This wasn't supposed to happen. She searched their faces, but they looked away. Surely someone would smile at her after what she'd been through? And then she was being steered towards the Parents' Room; aware she was hearing the words she dreaded most.

'I'm so sorry, Mrs Bound. I'm afraid things didn't go so well for your wee one.'

'What happened?'

The nurse swallowed hard. 'As we applied the nitrous oxide anaesthesia, Katia started fitting. The surgeons managed to massage her heart back and decided to continue. On opening her chest cavity, it was discovered her major blood vessels were misrouted into and out of her heart. Sadly, on closing it, her heart became sluggish again before finally stopping. I'm afraid there was nothing we could do.'

Someone handed Ayda a bag, a very small bag containing some familiar items: a blue dress and a shawl — her daughter's possessions — so little to show for such a precious life.

Ayda was left alone. And hours later, rising from the floor of the Parents' Room, she left the hospital and walked home.

In her bedchamber, she clutched the tiny dress, an empty bottle of gin lying beside her. *Mother's ruin* she thought, except the gin wasn't to blame. Pulling back the curtains, the birds had already started their joyful chorus as crimson and azure streaked across the sky. A yellow ball was rising from the horizon ready for the new day, the sky more beautiful than she had ever seen before. Feeling for the bottle, a tremor rose through her body unleashing a fury she didn't know she possessed. Moments later, glass lay smashed against the concrete below, the shattering sounds disturbing the servants' preparations for the day.

Her maid found her scratched and bleeding.

'How can the sun just rise like that?' Ayda sobbed. 'How can another day start as if nothing's happened, as if she didn't mean anything?'

Bintie wrapped her arms around Ayda tightly. 'That's just the way of the world, Miss.'

'How can everything carry on — without her?'

CHAPTER 23

During the last days of September 1917, spent and hollow, Ayda finally managed to leave her bedchamber. Immersed in a mosaic of colour: greens, yellows, and puce-reds, the vegetables from her walled garden surrounded her, while borders of quince, apple, gooseberry, and her favourite blackcurrant trees, grew in abundance. Heady scents of straw and floral notes wafted in the breeze, making her nose twitch. It was here she came for peace, solace and to read all the daily condolences which kept arriving for Adam, with the occasional one for little Katia. Though well-meaning, the words felt empty, meaningless, and few penetrated the mantle of her grief. Picturing the people, her acquaintances from long ago, she flicked through a few carelessly.

As if summoned to account for himself, tidings in a thick spider-scrawl landed in her lap from Cameron Muir.

Dear Ayda,

Sincerest commiserations, my girl, you've really had a time of it, though for your own good, I recommend you stay busy. I can tell you for nothing, if you were back at the War Office, you'd not have a moment to wallow in life's misfortunes.

We've been requisitioning like there's no tomorrow (and perhaps there isn't?). Ammunition, guns, more ammunition, even tanks, for goodness' sake, which are the new obsession. Great big, lumbering monstrosities always breaking down or sinking in the mud. And aeroplanes too, so many of your potty planes that my in-tray bulges with orders. There's so much happening here I hardly know how I will cope.

My secretary is dim-witted, almost illiterate, and innumerate, with fewer skills in her entire body than in just one of your fingers. And here's the rub now, Ayda: as you'll no doubt be wondering what to do with yourself, well, how about joining me? I could do with someone of your calibre, with your skills. Please give it some thought. Sorry again for your losses.

Respectful wishes,

Cameron Muir

Though Mr Muir's letter had come close to a compliment, it didn't make Ayda want to pack her bags and spring back into action, and she resented his suggestions about her future, however well intentioned. People should let her decide what to do in her own time. There was no real need to care for anyone now because there was no one left to care for.

The letters just made her feel even lonelier. She opened the final one. It was from Adam's brother, Granville.

Ayda,

No doubt you have been anticipating correspondence regarding my late brother's estate. As the present Lord Bound, I am duty-bound in this respect as both executor and legal guardian of all assets pertaining to him.

It has been brought to my attention that over a period of time, you have been parading yourself as Mrs Adam Bound and signing documentation to this effect. If you persist in using my family's name, I will prosecute. Your shabby marriage is neither legal nor binding owing to my brother's state of mind at the time of its sad occurrence. This is further evidenced by medical assessments obtained from his Squadron's C.O. and from the Chief Medical Officer. It is my opinion that you tricked and bamboozled a weak, confused man for your own gain and as such, Miss Gulzar, you are an evil fortune-hunter.

The Bound family has a proud, pure lineage stretching back to Tudor times, a fact my late brother always appreciated. Any attempts to contaminate it by marriage to someone such as yourself, can only be construed as the desperate act of a mad man or at the very least, a cry for help. It is my belief that the realisation of his actions may have contributed to his unfortunate and premature demise. Rest assured; my lawyers will prove your marriage lacks validity.

However, under the circumstances, I am prepared to be extremely charitable on condition you sever all contact. I have drawn up papers for my late brother's London home, Audley House, to be transferred to your name, Ayda Gulzar, along with its full complement of staff. In addition, you will be provided with an income of one thousand pounds per year. These are generous terms, but if you so much as step foot at Dunthorpe House, the agreement will cease with immediate effect.

As you may know, part of my home has been requisitioned by the War Office, and is now a military hospital. In these sad times, it is proving a valuable contribution to the war effort. Your mother had been residing there but she was causing concern. Confused and unable to communicate in English, she has been distressing both patients and staff. We have sent her to St Catherine's convent in Ealing, where the nuns have agreed to look after her.

I now wish to terminate contact between the Bound estate and yourself,
Lord Granville Bound

Fists clenched and shaking with rage, Ayda's eyes smarted again. How dare he imply that Adam hadn't been of sound mind or that their marriage wasn't legal. But he had. That was Granville!

In a very short time, she'd learned a lot about Adam's brother, none of it very pleasant. His letter was nothing more than an elaborate exercise in bluff and bluster to scare her because she knew her marriage's validity. She had a marriage certificate ready for any solicitor to see. Still, she didn't feel up to dealing with Granville at the moment, and had no appetite for legal wrangles until she'd fully recovered from her losses.

She glanced through the newspapers that had built up in her absence. She learned that the Allies were still engaged at the Third Battle of Ypres, that Scarborough had been bombed by submarines, and that moonlight air raids had returned. Just then, a whirring sound from the powder-puff clouds above disturbed her, a small plane bouncing into view. Inspecting its neat lines, she saw it was a Nieuport 17 — the same plane Adam had met his death in.

She looked back down and saw a short, scribbled note that she had missed. It was from Captain Bonneville. Ayda had met with him on a handful of occasions, always liking his easy, unassuming manner. Based at Upavon, he had directed her work both at Farnborough and the Central, and kept in contact during her absence. His words, though brief, were well chosen: *When you are ready, Ayda, please contact me. Your oily family will be here waiting for you. Contact and away, my dear. Captain Bonneville.*

And he was right.

'I think I'll go back to flying,' she muttered to herself.

Immediately, the leaves swayed their approval, but then Bintie arrived with another bundle of letters. Ayda noticed the one on top was postmarked Oxfordshire. There was only one person she knew there…

The envelope contained two letters. As expected, one was from Thomas Shuttleby, and the other one, enclosed, was again from her brother-in law, but addressed to Thomas. She read that letter first.

Dear Mr Shuttleby,

I am writing to you as the present Lord Bound regarding items littering the outbuildings of my estate.

Various bits of mechanical detritus require immediate removal as we attempt to provide appropriate medical stores for our burgeoning hospital. It may have escaped your notice but our country is at war. The Bound family have answered the call of duty in full, with Dunthorpe House now a military hospital — unlike some, we Bounds do not shirk responsibility. I note, however, that your home Polworth, still houses your family's furniture business, advertising its good fortune to all, despite the present climate.

Your possessions here are also evidence, sadly, of how delusional my late brother had become (with your help), and furthermore document the beginning of his decline into insanity. Therefore, their immediate removal is required. Failure to do so will leave me no option but to eject them by whichever means I see fit.

Yours faithfully,

Lord Granville Bound

Granville had indeed been busy, and Ayda wondered at the gall of the man. It was bad enough he'd written to her, but to be so rude to one of Adam's friends, too? And the martyred way he mentioned Dunthorpe House was now a military hospital was really beginning to rile. Naturally, it wouldn't have escaped his notice that by doing so would substantially reduce death duties after his father, had perished. Ayda took a deep breath and opened the second, longer letter:

My dearest Ayda,

Only now can I bring myself to write and offer my sincerest condolences for your double loss. I can only imagine the heartbreak you must be feeling.

I have been home on leave attempting to arrange accommodation for the collection (please see Lord Bound's letter). I do not suppose you have any sway with your brother-in-law? Any suggestions would be gratefully received as I am not confident all the machines would survive the upheaval to Oxfordshire — this dreadful war has made us terribly neglectful.

Ayda paused, thinking it a blessing Thomas didn't know how things stood between herself and Granville. But the thought of Adam's beloved, now neglected Blackburn brought fresh tears to her eyes … and an idea that Audley House might accommodate them. She continued reading Thomas's letter.

I must tell you something which will come as a shock — I am no longer with the R.F.C.

No more falling from the sky without a parachute for me. I'm a mechanic now with the Royal Tank Regiment, terra firma and all that. And if this damned war ever ends, I'll go back to fixing motor cars. I'm off to north Belgium in three weeks' time. Believe it or not, tanks aren't that different from planes. An engine's an engine when all is said and done.

A chill like frost ran down her back. Where was Thomas heading? There'd been dreadful accounts of the New Zealanders at Passchendaele in north Belgium, the rainfall so massive that even tanks weren't getting through, and those trapped inside were described as *meat in a tin can…* Clutching the paper, she continued.

Like I said, terra firma is what I want now. Even mud will do, not like those poor sods in the sky — so I wonder, dear Ayda, are you still a poor aviator?

Whatever you are doing, please look after yourself, and know you are in my thoughts. If you are able to write to me when I join the tankers, I would be most grateful.

Sincerest wishes, Thomas

Later that evening, Ayda penned a letter to Captain Bonneville mentioning she wished to return to work, though the thought made her stomach lurch. Was she returning to flying too soon? A full-length dressing glass stood before her under the window of a moonless sky, the mirrored glass drawing her in.

'I am a widow,' she told her reflection. 'A widow like many others. And my baby daughter died… Died.' Her breath steamed the cold surface as she repeated the words over and over again, telling herself they were true, wondering if she would ever believe them, and knowing she had no choice.

CHAPTER 24

As the weeks of October 1917 slid into November, Ayda avidly read the papers Bintie brought for her, looking for news of Thomas. The Battle of Passchendaele featured more and more. Buoyant from their success at Vimy Ridge six months earlier, the Canadians had advanced north to the Ypres area of Belgium, arriving at Passchendaele to reinforce the New Zealanders. A fierce battle had unfolded. And by November 1917, casualty rates for the British had spiralled to around two hundred and fifty thousand, due to the appalling conditions.

A heavily censored note then arrived from Thomas, which, despite his obvious enthusiasm, failed to alleviate her fears.

Dearest Ayda,

Arrived in Belgium. First outing with the tankers! Landscape hostile. In a tank called BB. Glad I'm on the inside, but mud is still terra firma. Better than being up in the air, though I doubt you'll agree!

She didn't. Having followed news of the tankers daily, she now knew enough to track Thomas's progress: his tank was a F41 Mark IV nicknamed 'Bully Beef' — after the tinned corned beef supplied to the troops — en route from Hooge to Zonnebeke, though Bully Beef's sister tank, 'The Fray Bentos', had been stuck in No Man's Land for sixty hours during 'The Siege of Fray Bentos'. Shaking her head, she let out a sigh. What was he thinking? The papers hadn't minced their words either, an extract from the *Times* shocking her with its description of life at the front.

All around fighting is fierce with water lying across this low, flat land where casualties grow daily in the sinking mud. Drainage ditches have failed, and the rain falls from the sky at an alarming rate; quick, cold, and blinding like a barrage of arrows. Pity our men in this as Belgium faces its worst rainfall for seventy years. And after three years of heavy fighting, the battlefields resemble a mucous porridge of mud and sludge making conditions horrific. Again, pity our men. Every tree, house, church and road from Ypres to Zonnebeke, has been smashed to pieces, the whole stretch now a pungent cratered ocean of percolating mud which, as it moves, sucks in battle-weary men, trucks and horses. There is but one exception — with its treads carefully navigating the liquefied terrain, one tank carries on — Bully Beef. And sends its greetings from Passchendaele!

At Farnborough, Ayda was fighting a battle of her own. She had questioned her return to work, but as soon as she saw the planes lined up as if to greet her, she knew she was where she was meant to be. Something felt different though. The frisson of energy, the crazy rush that had previously whipped about the site had gone, but maybe grief had made her less receptive to it.

The factory chief, Mr Henry Fowler, a former railway engineer, looked at her glumly, a spotted handkerchief passing liberally over his bald head. Ayda noted his appearance had changed too: older, thinner and greyer.

'Good to have you back, Ayda,' he said.

'Well, it's good to be back,' she said. 'Thankfully nothing much here has changed?'

'Big changes here, I'm afraid, Ayda. We've had a real time of it. All the designers have left. Henry Follond too.' He pointed upwards to a plane. 'And this is our last in-house prototype.'

Ayda looked up at the test pilot. It was at one thousand feet, and she examined it with growing horror: its shape, outline, and design all made it nose- and tail-heavy, and she knew this never would have been allowed before.

What was going on? An idea was beginning to form at the back of her mind. The machine looked dreadful — not worthy of a Farnborough prototype; it was diving now, and she knew she must look away.

'Looks like you'll need a second prototype,' she said, struggling to keep her voice from shaking in anger.

'Thought we'd sorted the torque out, but I'm not convinced. Look at it, it's all over the place and the directional control is impossible. We've had a terrible time since January, Ayda. You've heard about Major Frank Goodden?'

'No.'

'End of January it was. Only ten minutes into the flight, the port wing cellule collapsed at about a thousand feet. The plane just broke up, fell out of the sky and crashed. Best test pilot we've ever had. Been with us on and off since 1914. Only twenty-seven. Such a loss.' Mr Fowler clenched his fists. 'Something else is afoot here too, Ayda, and it's not just down to these new Aero Acceptance Parks. Trenchard's not saying much either, but more's happening in the New Year. Testing will be moved. And we've only got one project in the pipeline for March: an A.E.3 armoured two-seat pusher, hardly a world beater, eh? Not even designed here.'

Ayda knew several Aero Acceptance Parks had sprung up to ease Farnborough's burden of assembling, storing and flight-testing machines. 'Surely, the Parks are a good thing; I mean, a year ago Farnborough couldn't cope. Change is inevitable. Making everything better, faster and more efficient, that's the nature of aviation today, surely?' She pulled a face. 'Though I'd be heartbroken if Farnborough changed too much or…' Her earlier euphoria had completely evaporated; replaced by foreboding.

The year had brought too much change already and Farnborough was the only stable thing left in her life. She had hungered for this busy, bustling place, full of people and planes, and couldn't bear to see her memories vanish.

Mr Fowler patted her hand as she stared into the distance, feeling more like a fractious child than a successful pilot.

'Look, Ayda, no one's taking Farnborough away. How could they? It's too big.' He paused. 'Do you remember your first week? How big and crazy everything was? God knows, it couldn't have carried on like that.'

She exhaled, her shoulders relaxing. His words were having an effect. 'Just so long as there are still planes for me to transport, I don't really mind.'

'Of course,' he said. 'Production is still at capacity. We can't get the planes to the schools and over to France quick enough, so we're very grateful for your assistance … especially after your run of bad luck, my dear. I hope you don't mind, Ayda, but Captain Bonneville mentioned it to me when he organised your visit today.'

Before she could answer, a sickening whine from the sky made them both look up. A wingless dark object in freefall plummeted to the ground, coming to rest only yards from the entrance. Soon a mushroom of thick grey smoke enveloped the air around it.

Ayda had seen enough. The last few months came rushing back: Adam, the baby, now this. It was all too soon.

Death, and more death wherever she went or looked, there was no escape.

It had to stop.

Suddenly everything around her began to spin. The sky … the hangars …

She felt herself sinking; the ground rushing up to meet her as she fell towards it. A thin flapping material engulfed her, a strange roughness against her fingers. Then someone tried sitting her up, passing her a hot cup of tea. They were being kind. A sickly acrid smell of burning fuel, fuselage and flesh made her turn her face away. People were rushing everywhere as the fire engine arrived at the wreckage.

'Thank God for the old balloon canvas, eh?' Mr Fowler said, looking concerned. 'Cushioned your fall.'

Ayda allowed her eyes to close, thinking of the plane and its burning pilot. It made her think of Thomas Shuttleby wanting solid ground, not wanting to fall from the sky. She fingered the canvas, feeling its strength as it sat spread across the ground, and a conviction she had had many times returned to her now. She would use her intellect to stop further tragedy. If she could fly and plan and design planes, then surely she could help stop such things from happening?

At Roehampton Airfield, Ayda sought out head designer, Everard Calthrop. A former railway engineer, he was a slight man with a most stupendous moustache who had patented his first parachute in 1913. The R.F.C. were then offered all his designs. And all were rejected.

'Sorry for your loss, Miss Ayda,' Calthrop began awkwardly. 'And thank you for your interest in helping with the parachutes, but I'm beginning to think they'll never take them… I'm sorry for it because they might even have prevented Adam's…'

Ayda raised a hand to stop him. 'It's not your fault, Mr Calthrop, I know how stubborn the Corps can be.' She knew better than most, and yes, Adam had paid the price.

Calthrop shook his head. 'But I'm not staying quiet anymore. I've started publicising. The ballooners have them now. It's madness. Even the Germans want my designs because they're safe, and they work!'

'I know,' Ayda said, bile in her throat as she recalled the R.F.C.'s regulations. 'But you must understand, ballooners are a different category, Mr Calthrop. Airmen are ten-a-penny.'

They walked across the grass approaching a black mushroom of canvas from which a man crawled out.

'The R.F.C. are getting more ridiculous by the minute. Did you hear about my seat?'

'Your ejector-seat?' Ayda's eyes widened. 'Yes, what a marvellous idea to use compressed air.'

'Turned their noses up at it last year, would you believe?'

They continued walking, eyes focussed on a second man who had just jumped from the gondolier, and who was now suspended below a huge floating umbrella.

'This one will be ready in the new year. They'll have to take them then because now the undercover teams are interested.'

'I'll believe it when I see it, Mr Calthrop, but I'm happy to help — calculations, designs, whatever you need.'

Calthrop ran to meet his test pilot, and shouted back over his shoulder. 'I'm calling this one the *Guardian Angel* — what do you think?'

Struggling to smile, Ayda felt a chill return, remembering Adam talk of guardian angels, and hoping now things would be different.

CHAPTER 25

Over Christmas, Ayda finally found the strength to visit her mother. She knew it was long overdue, but she couldn't cope with the grief of seeing Rosina so altered, on top of everything else she had been going through. Uncertain of what she would find when she reached St Catherine's convent, she blinked at the meandering path ahead of her. Beautifully kept flowerbeds encircled a marble statue of the Madonna along the convent's approach. The statue's perfect white hands stretched out in welcome, red rosary bead spiralling around marble fingers.

Ayda opened the door at the entrance and the brightness disappeared. There was no one around to greet her, so she chose one of the long corridors stretching out in front of her. At the end, a single candle illuminated a stone staircase.

An elderly nun hurried to welcome her from behind it and Ayda explained she was there to see Rosina. Smiling sweetly through crooked teeth, the nun led her to the top floor and ushered her into the first room on the right, before leaving Ayda and Rosina alone.

Rosina sat motionless in a chair below a barred window. The whitewashed walls were bare apart from a wooden crucifix nailed above the bed.

'*Ciao, Mama. Come stai?*' Ayda said anxiously.

There was no response. Rosina's black eyes stared ahead of her; she did not react to Ayda's touch.

'Mama, I bring bad tidings,' Ayda said in English. 'A lot has happened since I last saw you. Do you remember Adam?'

Rosina's eyes flickered briefly but still she said nothing. Ayda trailed off. Any thought of confiding in her mother was gone.

The door opened and the nun returned. Rosina smiled and reached out her hands. The nun took them and stroked them, murmuring soothing words.

'She doesn't remember me, does she?' Ayda asked.

The nun shook her head, sadly.

Hours later, sobbing into a pot of tea, Ayda was reflecting on her visit when loud noises disturbed her. The front door to Audley House was pounded with considerable force. Peering from behind the bedroom curtain, she spied the figure of Lord Granville Bound in the street below: his lean body and arrogant tilt of the head was unmistakeable. Before she could call out to instruct the maids to leave him outside, the front door was opened.

'Where is she?' she heard him yell.

Before long, Ayda heard his steps and Granville stumbled into her bedchamber.

She held her breath as she heard him moving around. From her hiding place, she sent a heartfelt thank you to her late husband. He had sent detailed descriptions of all the nooks and crannies in the house and she had spent time exploring them and discovering her current secret hideaway. Granville had never cared for this house. It had been Adam's and now it was hers.

Ayda peered out from behind a tiny gap in a marble-veined mock fireplace and watched as her inebriated brother-in-law became increasingly agitated, calling her every name under the sun. He clawed the walls like an animal, throwing her clothes out of the window and kicking the furniture, before he tripped over and landed with a thud below the mahogany bedstead.

Ayda studied the rise and fall of his chest, his face so like and unlike her husband's. There an emptiness lurked which wasn't just attributable to Granville's callous nature. Devoid of imagination, patience or compassion, his features had no spark, no intelligence or kindness, and that, she decided, was the difference.

After what seemed like an hour but was likely only ten minutes, she crept out from behind her stone hideaway. Granville was snoring loudly now, clearly in a drunken stupor. She didn't want to risk being here when he woke up. She quickly gathered her flying clothes and called for a cab, which soon arrived to take her to the Cavendish, the hotel near the R.F.C. Club where she'd spent the night before her wedding.

When Ayda received word from Bintie that Granville had left, she returned to Audley House. Fortunately, he had not returned since. She kept a bag packed, just in case, but she was hopeful his outburst was enough and she wouldn't see him again.

The war had now entered its fourth year. She had been working hard on designing the parachutes with Calthrop which had felt good, challenging her brain with experimentation and calculations. She had begun to feel hopeful again that there could be a better future ahead if the R.F.C. could be convinced to take note and start using the parachutes, but now she really wanted to get back to flying. It was time to recapture the life she had before her tragic losses.

And her orders had come through, too — with a surprise. Captain Bonneville had recommended a new airfield with new people — fitting, he said, for the new chapter in her life. So, on 1st February 1918, Ayda headed to London Colney Airfield. It was time to lay the ghosts of her past to rest.

Differing in size from Farnborough and the Central, the aerodrome at Shenleybury had started life as a R.F.C. safe landing area, and, with its farm and twenty-five acres, had recently expanded into two parts. With three permanent hangars on its eastern side, it also housed three temporary Bessonneau hangars on its north side, where a group of American pilots had settled and begun training.

Ayda was today due to meet the new C.O. This wasn't normal procedure, but apparently the C.O. liked a more personal approach, to explain his reasoning and motivations to his complete team so they would know what to expect.

Approaching his office, an odd fluttering in her stomach told her she was nervous, but she wasn't entirely sure why. She dearly hoped this C.O. wouldn't object to a woman on the dispatch team.

Ayda knocked on the door and waited. When there was no response, she slowly turned the handle and pushed the door open. The room was empty. Outside, two dispatch pilots sat smoking their pipes. She headed in their direction, wondering how long she should wait. She thought of Captain Bonneville, what he would say? Her duties were clear: always remain on the periphery of a squadron, work on the planes but never make contact with the pilots, only occasionally with mechanics — and never with a Commanding Officer, which is why she had found being summoned by him so strange.

Ayda's gaze then moved to a group of men as they snaked up and down the airfield in a line. At the helm, a sandy head bobbed up and down, standing a full head above the rest. In and out of the first three hangars weaved the khaki-clad line, the men hanging on to their leader's every move, passing the last hangar before the mechanics' quarter. There, the leader suddenly halted, almost causing a domino effect.

The group had stopped near where Ayda was waiting and she felt even more out of place standing amongst the jocular men. Sauntering along the assembled ranks, the sandy-headed man pretended to hand something to each pilot as he wound an imaginary device. Halfway down the line he stopped, looking over in Ayda's direction.

'All latecomers welcome,' he said, smiling. 'Just step right up. This way for tickets, all tickets please!' His voice was deep, mellow, the words softly spoken, and Ayda found herself mesmerised.

'Get your tickets for the R.F.C.!' he shouted. 'That's the Royal Flying *Circus*. Step right up to see Old Man Hun himself. This way please.'

Peals of laughter from the men encouraged him more.

'It'll be quite a trip, probably just one-way but never mind, the company will be good. Step this way to avoid disappointment.' His long arms waved, and the pilots gathered round, then someone was propelled forwards, narrowly missing him.

'Oh, I say, sorry, sir, Major Randal.'

Ayda looked up. She'd heard this name before. And suddenly she remembered all about Randal, Adam's best friend at 39a Squadron. A pair of deep blue eyes settled on her, belonging to the new C.O., Major Rick Randal.

The dispatch pilot meeting was brief and somewhat rushed after the morning's festivities. Ayda stood slightly back, flanked by her two larger colleagues. Major Randal looked both serious and confused, seemingly unsure as to why he'd called the meeting.

'I am angry,' he said, clearing his throat. 'All the S.E.5's you have so dutifully delivered here over the last few weeks have been compromised. They were fitted with a ridiculous celluloid windscreen rather like a greenhouse. Now I've nothing against greenhouses in gardens, but not on S.E.5a's. They get in the way, skewer my gunsight, so I can't see where I'm going. Also, they're too sharp and in a crash they could easily cut a pilot's face and arms.' He looked around at Ayda and the two other dispatch pilots. 'This will mean a lot of extra work for you three, more to-ing and fro-ing, so I do apologise, but I have the support of Farnborough in my decision. The fighting efficiency of my men cannot be impaired in any way, so back they must go! Any questions?'

The room fell silent apart from the C.O.'s foot tapping. Ayda suddenly found herself talking. She never would have done this a year ago, but now she knew she must. She knew what she was talking about, her confidence had come from experience.

'I wonder, sir, if I might suggest a further modification? The telescopic gunsight used isn't suitable for the S.E.5. For starters, at thirty inches, it's too large and has a terrible habit of collecting oil on the forward lens.' She could feel the C.O.'s eyes boring into her, challenging her, and felt she must continue. 'I discussed this once with someone who flew Nieuports, and we concluded that the Aldis gunsight was suitable for Nieuports, *not* for S.E.'s. I told him I couldn't see a thing, that I was glad I never had to find the enemy nor shoot at close range with it. He agreed. And I never knew an occasion when his judgement was wrong.'

The major nodded and confirmed that yes, the Aldis would be replaced with a Vickers ring sight. The meeting quickly ended, and the C.O. drifted outside to be mobbed by more pilots.

It hadn't been that bad, Ayda thought, as the butterflies in her stomach fluttered away. She was impressed by what she had seen so far of Major Rick Randal.

CHAPTER 26

Ayda put down the newspaper. The Royal Flying Corps and the Royal Naval Air Service were to merge. It was about time! For years they'd be squabbling over funds, staff, equipment, training, recognition; then a distinguished ex-Boer veteran, General Jan Smuts, was invited to report on Britain's Air Defence, and in particular how it could gain supremacy. His recommendations in August 1917 concluded an independent air force was needed, independent of both Army and Navy. And on 1st April 1918, the Royal Air Force was born — the first of its kind. Ever.

Months earlier, Lord Northcliffe's article in the *Daily Mail* entitled *Our Unknown Air Heroes* had caused a stir, demanding whether or not this new brand of hero should be recognised. With their profile raised, praise followed, then finally adulation:

What I want to know, Ayda had read, *is why an Englishman whose hobby is bringing down sky Huns in braces and trios between luncheon and tea, who can already claim a bag of 30 enemy aircraft, should have to wait and be killed before a grateful nation waiting to acclaim him could even learn his name? I wonder if people in England realise that the German Air Service is the most popular and feted branch of the Kaiser's war machine because German authorities have imagination to exploit its personal side. How many people in these islands can name as many British Airmen as fingers on one hand?*

The formation of the new R.A.F. ensured the attention placed on the pilots continued, and Ayda received an invitation to its inaugural celebrations, not for her own flying abilities, but as the widow of Captain Adam Bound D.S.O., M.C. Despite the personal snub, she felt honoured for his sake.

The celebrations were to take place at the new headquarters of the R.A.F at the site of the Cecil Hotel, a grand hotel between the Thames Embankment and the Strand. A few days later, stepping through its entrance, Ayda quickly noticed her first ace, and a very well-known one too. The diminutive figure of James McCudden was attending, after recently receiving his Victoria Cross at Buckingham Palace for conspicuous bravery, exceptional perseverance, keenness and very high devotion to duty. Stealing a sideways glance, Ayda thought he looked uncomfortable in the limelight, and he appeared more like a kindly curate than a killing machine. Whatever it was that made him one of the most successful aces, wasn't immediately apparent.

Everyone, it seemed, was curious about these famous aces, thanks to the *Daily Mail*'s article, and the adulation of these pilots continued well into the night. As the drink flowed and the jokes became bawdier, Ayda decided to leave, not wishing to find herself in awkward circumstances.

The public soon demanded that aces' scores were broadcasted. This was a step too far for Ayda, as, after all, these scores were nothing more than a tally of death. How would such publicity help the R.A.F., she wondered? It would only add pressure on the men and turn their jobs into a race or a competition, making them more likely to take risks and end up dead, like Adam.

A week later, Ayda returned to Hertfordshire and London Colney at the head of a fleet of modified S.E.5a's. Now at the end of their training, she was curious to see how 65a Squadron was shaping up under the watchful eye of Major Randal. A strange euphoria hung over the airfield, but today grief gripped at her tightly and she was unable to shake it off. She knew Adam would have enjoyed the recent R.A.F. celebrations, and she had been thinking of him a lot. Here at London Colney, she felt exposed. At least at Farnborough, she could hide in one of the many hangars and be swallowed up by the airfield's massive size.

Recently her workload had made socialising impossible, even if her brief had allowed it. For the first time, she felt envious of the camaraderie and banter that existed between the male pilots. A chilly wind whipped at her hair, and a rumble of low-flying S.E.5's made her look up. Minutes later, four biplanes flew across the airstrip, pelting bananas at targets ten feet apart. Shouts and laughter sounded. Pilots then spilled out, counting the bananas, before it was unanimously agreed Major Randal had hit the most. Ayda glanced at the targets — all were images of the German ace, Manfred von Richthofen.

What was going on? 65a was supposed to be an elite fighting squadron. Remembering the office's supply of newspapers, she headed there to see what she had missed. A headline from the American tabloid *The New York Times* caught her eye: *FOE'S GREATEST ACE KILLED: Baron von Richthofen Shot Down After 80th Victory Had Been Claimed for Him.*

Was this true? The mechanics would know and she did have a repaired propeller shaft to collect. As she neared the hangar, she heard animated voices. She burst in.

'Sorry, Miss Ayda,' Private Matthews, the younger mechanic, reddened. 'Bit busy today, head's all-a-swimming with everything that's going on, forgot about your propeller shaft.'

She smiled sweetly. 'Something up?'

'Nobody told you yet, Miss Ayda? Never mind. Got it first-hand from the Major after he'd telephoned the C.O. in Brown's squadron.'

'Brown?'

'Captain Roy Brown, Canadian. Supposed to have killed Richthofen.' Matthews caught his breath. 'Major Randal's read the official report and what a story!'

She caught his excitement. This was momentous. 'Do tell. I want to hear every last detail.'

'That's just what the Major said. Told me he got every detail because he wanted to know Richthofen had suffered, that he knew it was his time.'

She screwed up her face. Major Randal's loathing of the Germans was often a topic of conversation.

Matthews continued. 'Major Randal said it had looked at one point like any one of a dozen were after him, that he needed to know which lucky bugger got him. Said he was bellowing down the telephone piece: *Who was the blighter? Tell me! I'd have traded my M.C. for a pop at the pig.*'

'And did he find out?'

'It's confusing,' the mechanic admitted. 'The Canadians are sticking to their story, claiming it was their boy, Roy Brown, but the Aussies are becoming very vocal now. Said it was their rifles, so who to believe?'

Ayda soaked in the information, forgetting about her propeller shaft, imagining Cappy Airfield and the Somme swirling in a haze of early morning mist — the German ace resplendent in red leather — her eyes bright and feverish, feeling as if she'd been there too. She often felt like this, as if transported to France: taking off on a blast of smoke and burn as the squadron tore out over the Channel, deep blue sea below, grey skies above, often feeling tension in her hands when they spotted the first enemy plane out of the haze. But this tale was different. She was shocked at how the tale had sucked her in, how much it mattered that the German ace had been killed.

'It's not surprising the Major's so interested,' Matthews said. 'He's a top ace himself now, up there with 'Mick' Mannock and Jimmy McCudden. Shot down more Huns than poor old Albert Ball, God rest his soul.'

'Major Randal is an ace?'

Matthews nodded. 'You only need five kills to call yourself an ace, and the Major has a lot more than that.'

Ayda smiled. That made Adam officially an ace too with his eight victories. This neither pleased nor displeased her, knowing he would have felt the same. Killing was never his reason for flying, unlike some, and she felt ashamed of her earlier hunger and enthusiasm for the story of the killing of the German ace. Adam, Rick Randal, Richthofen, they were all the same, just on different sides. She wondered if there was a Frau Richthofen feeling grief-stricken, like her, and whether Rick Randal appreciated that he was alive, while Adam and Richthofen were dead.

CHAPTER 27

Ayda had had enough. Each time she landed at London Colney her inspection checks were rushed through. It felt like someone wanted her out as soon as she landed, and speaking with her fellow dispatch pilots, they were having no such problems. Surely the C.O. could see how she was being treated. So, why was he allowing this?

She remembered again how highly Adam had thought of Rick Randal, so was she being unreasonable? No, because as C.O., he should be above pettiness. There was nothing for it. She would have to confront him. Even though the rules of her engagement were clear — no contact with squadron pilots — she had her safety to consider, and her pride.

Approaching his office that afternoon, butterflies were again fluttering about her stomach, which annoyed her. Apart from his many citations and Adam's praise, Randal wasn't a typical C.O. His behaviour was more than a little eccentric, though the men seemed to respond well to it.

As she approached his office, the doorknob turned and the major emerged.

'Ayda,' he said, looking into her face. 'I'm so sorry, I hadn't realised up until now that you are the widow of Captain Adam Bound. My sincerest apologies. I wondered if you would like me to tell you something of our time serving together?'

Ayda froze, her resentment vanishing. Up close, his face was more handsome than she'd realised, and his smile was warmer than she remembered. Before she'd even realised it, he'd taken hold of her hand and it felt good … very good.

Over the following weeks, they took their breaks together most days and would walk around the airfield. They had long, comfortable conversations, mostly about Adam.

Today, they were walking in silence. Oily fumes hung heavy in the air, noisy engines hiding summer sounds. Rick's steps in rhythm with Ayda's strides, they headed down a winding path beyond the hangars near Shenleybury Lane, out to open fields. Ayda broke the silence with an update on her work: 'I've delivered the last modification. A few more days with the mechanics, some paperwork, then I pack up and leave this Friday.'

Rick nodded. 'We've received our orders as well. We leave for France next week.'

Ayda's stomach contracted. She had grown to like, and even care, for Rick, and she couldn't bear the thought of him leaving. Inside her pockets, her hands were trembling. She was scared.

Rick continued on, unaware. 'Can I ask you why you do it, why you still fly?' He turned to face her, his eyes searching. 'I mean, it's not like you have to — like we do.'

'A couple of reasons, really. First, I enjoy flying immensely, I love it more than anything. It's never scared or worried me. And second, of course, Adam wanted me to.'

'Really?' Rick raised an eyebrow. 'He probably wouldn't want you to if he'd known how things would end. And anyway, I'd have thought you'd have stopped after what happened to him.'

'Actually, no,' she said, pursing her lips. 'You don't understand. Adam went to a lot of trouble arranging work for me. Without him where would I be? Probably teaching to an empty classroom. I owe it to him to continue flying, but I've also worked very hard for this, proved my worth over and over again. So, no, I won't just give it up because it's dangerous.

Sometimes we *have* to face danger when it's the right thing to do.'

Rick stood silent for a moment. 'I think you'll find I *do* understand. Without Adam, I dread to think where *I'd* be too. Not Major Randal, Commanding Officer of 65a Squadron, that's for sure! I was an outsider, not on the usual public school-R.F.C. gravy train. No one liked me. He believed in me, looked out for me. Without Adam, I'd probably be fertilising some corner of France.'

Looking up at his towering frame, she remembered how Adam had spoken of Rick. Thinking of her own background, her servant mother; she realised Adam must have enjoyed supporting the underdog, knowing his family had always treated him much like one.

Rick's expression clouded. 'He always seemed so confident, and he was so happy that day — I couldn't believe it when we heard his Nieuport had disintegrated…'

'Stop! Please!' Ayda grasped his hands. They felt warm despite her growing chill. And very alive. But she couldn't talk about Adam's death, not to him.

'I'm sorry.' He squeezed her hands gently, before quickly releasing them and turning away.

Relieved, she let out a breath. It was too soon. Friendship, yes, but nothing more — she had no intention of grieving for another man, she told herself, as the winding path to the airfield came into view.

This time Rick spoke first, changing the subject.

'We're keen to go back to the front. This publicity, this fame malarkey, isn't helping. Makes it impossible for us pilots to go about our own business. McCudden's suffering the most because of his V.C. Hardly been out at all, apart from a stint at Number 1 Aerial in Ayr.'

'How are you coping?'

'Fine, and as Mannock would say, *it's all just piffle,*' Rick said. 'But I am worried about McCudden. He's convinced his fame is working against him. Mannock's been given 74 Squadron, I'm off next week with 65a, but McCudden's got nothing. And he's itching to go.'

'Perhaps they're resting him, making sure he's ready?'

'I wish I could believe you, but no one knows what to think.' Rick sighed, kicking a few stones.

The air felt fresh with meadowsweet smells after the choking carburettor fumes. 'Maybe he should change duties; after all, he is an excellent mechanic.'

'The best, but that's not likely. Anyway, I hope he gets something soon.'

'I could write to him, if you like, see if he is all right?'

'But, Mrs Bound — Ayda — I thought that perhaps you might write to me!'

The first hangar loomed ahead, and they both smiled, the air suddenly clearer despite the fumes.

CHAPTER 28

21st May 1918

Dearest Ayda,

Thank you for your letter. My apologies for the delay in replying. We are well settled here at C with much activity around. Am reminded to write tonight as there's a clear, starlit sky and someone close to both our hearts would, I know, under different circumstances be out watching through his telescope. It is said the best view of the stars is from heaven — hopefully he is watching now!

Very intense here. Only yesterday, I chased nine planes singlehandedly for miles over B, but none would engage. Have lost a few pilots in the last week, R and V, and we've given up hope of finding P.

Yesterday, out at 10,000 feet we spotted two 2-seaters, and quickly dived on them, both were soon in flames. This afternoon, leading an OP in the same area, found two Pfalzs, and fired 40 rounds. Both went down. C says I can expect a bar to my D.S.O. So far have bagged around 50, only bettered by M and M!

Weather and visibility excellent so no chance of rest — please pray for rain! Lately not enjoying flying above 14,000 feet. Can't get to previous heights: head dizzy —hands and feet too cold. Also climb of bus here atrocious, needs attention. Mechanics not up to much. Am considering putting in for leave in late summer so don't make yourself too busy. Where will you be based? Perhaps you could clear your logbook?

Sincerely,

Your friend Rick

Logs sizzled on the fire as Ayda folded then unfolded Rick's letter. The flames warmed her chilled hands, heat radiating to her fingertips, as an idea began to form in her head. She began a letter, not to Rick but to James McCudden. As a time-served mechanic, she respected his opinion, though it would be *her* suggesting a solution rather than the other way around. The problem troubled many: high altitude flying caused anoxia — oxygen deprivation; both Adam and now Rick had complained of its effects, so she penned her ideas in the letter. A simple shutter or radiator vent would warm the cockpit with the heat from the engine, would he please try this? A few other modifications to improve the rate of climb were also included.

Ayda received McCudden's reply a week later.

Dear Ayda,

Thank you so much for your letter — very refreshing! We've both arrived at the same conclusion: the high compression pistons, the shortened exhaust pipe and the streamlining give me a fantastic climb — 10,000 feet in 9 minutes! And the radiator vent — warm feet and hands! I'm so glad you wrote making me test them else they'd still be on paper. It's wonderful you are so innovative.

Much appreciation,

James

A few days later Ayda was invited to speak at a meeting in celebration of the formation of the Women's Royal Air Force by its commandant, Violet Douglas-Pennant; the topic on which she was to speak was the mechanics of the S.E.5a. At first, Ayda had refused. Her dislike of meetings after Neptune Hall ran deep, but Miss Douglas-Pennant was very persuasive, and Ayda had finally come round to the idea when told the audience would be small, select and hand-picked.

In the smallest of hangars at Colney, a group of women assembled. Ayda's face paled as she surveyed the growing number. Not quite Neptune Hall, she thought, relieved, with its rows and rows of grey-haired men, but many more than she expected, and, looking out into the sea of faces, she wondered where the *small* and *select* audience came in.

The sound of a tea urn percolating distracted her, bringing a homely feel to the hangar amidst the oil and grease, and she calmed down enough to focus on what she would be saying. More and more chairs were laid out and women from everywhere came through the big sliding doors: drivers still in khaki or navy blue from both the Women's Army Auxiliary Corps and the Women's Royal Naval Service, many were in the new W.R.A.F. uniforms, along with motorcyclists, aircraft assembly workers, even cooks from the canteen. Ayda looked at them, and for a moment wondered how many of them could possibly join her — could learn to fly and be pilots given the chance. She suspected it was curiosity about *her* rather than about the S.E.5a's mechanics that drew her audience.

Violet Douglas-Pennant gave a brief address and introduction, stating that the W.R.A.F. would have its base at R.A.F. Flowerdown, a short distance away. At this, Ayda looked down, covering her eyeroll at the thought that it was probably selected because its name sounded most appropriate for women. But soon enough she was clearing her throat ready to begin, her fingers twitching uncontrollably behind her back.

'I thank you all for welcoming me here today to talk about the mechanics of an aircraft I have had the privilege of being acquainted with,' she began. 'As you know, it is making a significant difference to the men fighting. The S.E.5a was designed by three of Farnborough's best designers: Henry Folland, John Kenworthy and the late Major Frank Goodden. It has a geared 200 horsepower Hispano-Suiza V8 engine…'

There was movement in the audience. After five minutes on fuselage, wings, and the S.E.5's steerable tailskid, she moved on to diagrams and photographs, showing the plane's unique box-like appearance, hoping to hold their interest. The squirming continued. Even how the plane's synchronised Vickers gun had turned things around for the men fighting failed to inspire the audience, and now, even the drivers and motorcyclists in the front row and those with a modicum of military experience, looked bored.

Ayda looked around the hangar, her mouth dry — a change of tack was required. 'Some of you may have heard of Major James McCudden V.C. I had occasion to speak with him recently. A top ace but also an extremely competent mechanic, he tested some modifications we had talked about after pilots had complained of extreme cold and poor rates of climb…'

At the mention of McCudden, the audience looked marginally more interested, but soon enough boredom returned. Ayda cast her script aside, anger and disappointment flooding in. Couldn't they see how hard this was, how far she'd come from a shy, obedient girl standing on a pallet outside Neptune Hall, straining to hear what was being said? Here was an opportunity right under their noses to learn — a meeting laid on just for *women*.

'I suppose I should have come here today dressed in my sheepskin coat and salopettes, with my helmet, goggles and gauntlet gloves. But perhaps what you really want to know is how it feels to be in charge of take-off, landing, planning your route, doing your own checks, to be in control of your own destiny. Or in other words — how it feels to fly. The freedom, the exhilaration … let me tell you, ladies, flying feels good! No man can help you up there in the sky, nor a woman, for that matter — you are alone.'

Ayda glanced at her audience: the back row had now woken up, heads raised as if looking to the future.

'I came here today to tell you that it can be done. Women can fly, as I have done. Years ago, we would have never dreamt it possible — who could imagine our mothers' generation riding motorcycles, or driving cars and ambulances? We can do anything we want. I am proof of that ... and who knows what the future holds for us?'

She sat down to rousing applause, her cheeks burning, her heart racing. She had got there in the end.

CHAPTER 29

A week later, while re-reading Rick's first letter, Ayda noticed that a definite chill hovered over London despite his remarks on the heat across the Channel. She had replied to him and had been hoping for another letter, but so far, she had been disappointed. Absently tugging at her mass of dark brown hair, she wondered if she should cut it to a more manageable length? Stretching her mind back to the meeting, she knew many young women were opting for shorter cuts now, and that might make it easier to contain within her flying helmet.

Since her talk, she had frittered away a week sitting at home, waiting for work, thinking about Rick: like her, he'd had to work hard to get to where he was. Born without wealth or status, only with a spirit of adventure which often brought him close to disaster, he was a born leader, a brilliant pilot which Adam had often commented on. And she could no longer deny it. She felt a profound longing for him. A yearning which went beyond friendship. This shocked her.

Later, her curls fell away, clumping in little mounds at her feet, scissor blades click-clicking. Removing a small heart-shaped satin bag from a dresser, she put a solitary lock of hair inside. There it joined a wispier, darker lock and a lighter one of downy baby hair. Raising her hand to her newly cropped head, she stared into the looking glass at the unfamiliar image. *Who am I?*

Different Aydas appeared: Ayda the child: sitting alongside her mother, Ayda the pupil-teacher: in front of an abacus teaching her class. Then came Ayda the scientist: surrounded by Cameron Muir's papers and Adam's designs. Next, Ayda the secretary — very short-lived, followed quickly by Ayda the aviator — an infinite improvement. Finally, it was Ayda the wife and mother, neither role she could hold on to. And now only Ayda the aviator remained ... but soon, if Rick felt the same, then maybe Ayda the lover...

Teasing at her newly cropped hair, her colour rose and she shivered. A defiant face stared back at her, and she smiled.

After two weeks kicking her heels at home, Ayda knew she needed to mobilise, so she put in for a straightforward delivery on her most travelled route — Farnborough to Upavon. The day had started off well: a minimal south-westerly wind, the sun high in the powder-blue June sky, nothing looked out of place except perhaps the absence of a few fluffy clouds.

Her S.E.5a looked no different from its relatives: angular, boxy with its sawn-off nose. Keen to be airborne, Ayda had breezed through the pre-flight checks, noticing nothing untoward. Except this S.E.5a smelled different. As a rule, machines barely deviated from their usual list of oily smells or exhaust fumes and occasional wafts of pine or polish, but this machine had a faint acrid taint. What should she do? The machine was relatively young and its logbook showed regular services and no overuse. It was probably nothing. And it was *only* Farnborough to the Central, a route she had devoted near on two hundred hours of her life to. A waft of burnt toast tickled her nose. It was probably nothing, she repeated to herself, as she took off, easing back on the stick, climbing, then levelling out at a smooth eighty knots.

Flying at around three thousand feet, the S.E.5a's Hispano-Suiza engine hummed its way through the sky, the eddies of air currents and turbulence no real concern and after an hour of blissful flying, Ayda had quite forgotten the acrid scent.

Beginning a slow descent to the Central, she checked her speed, and looked over the side at familiar fields and farms forming below. Then three things happened at once: the wind direction suddenly changed, the oil pressure plummeted, and the plane shook as if having a fit of hiccups. The rattling of wings, struts, stick and rudder was accompanied by a vortex of turbulence in the cockpit, pulling at her helmet and goggles, lifting her head from her shoulders and almost suffocating her. The S.E.5a's nose dropped, and the noise of the wind became deafening: whistling through the wires, howling above any other sound. Why were there no vibrations, she wondered, and why had she never heard noise like this before?

Feeling strangely calm, the ghost-like silence of a stalled engine was almost soothing. Just as well, she thought, that Adam and Thomas had taught her how to glide using the principals of aerodynamics, learning how air and atmosphere interreact and mingle with objects around them. The principals of flight had come easily to her, she could always *feel* her way, feel what was needed, at one with the elements. She managed to glide her S.E.5a through the eddies of air and made a smooth landing in a nearby field.

Looking up from his cart, a farmer gaped as Ayda exited the cockpit, his pipe released so suddenly from his mouth that it tumbled to the ground. Ayda couldn't decide if it was the sudden appearance of the plane in his field or the sex of its pilot that disturbed him the most. Ayda threw off her goggles and helmet and cleared her throat, before smiling her widest, most winning smile.

'Apologies for the intrusion, sir, but can I catch a lift? My plane isn't working properly.'

Speech had deserted the farmer, although a low rumble in his throat eventually metamorphosised into words. The S.E.5a was then attached to the cart, and its fifteen-hundred-pound weight pulled the mile and a half to the Central by the wary horse.

Three hours late, and with the taciturn farmer handsomely rewarded, Ayda arrived at Captain Bonneville's office, tired by her ordeal.

'Terribly sorry for the late arrival, sir, but number 3210 is now safely delivered.' This wasn't strictly true because the lower wing's canvas fabric had ruptured in several places, but it all had been documented by Ayda.

Glancing at her report, Captain Bonneville raised a bushy eyebrow. 'A smell like burning toast, you say, Ayda? Well, I'll be damned if I can smell anything more than horse manure!'

CHAPTER 30

Ayda sat at home daydreaming. She was now in regular correspondence with Rick Randal and in all her time with Adam, she had never experienced such hopeless lovesickness, but something in Rick's letters resonated with her, and his words spoke to her very soul. She shook herself. *Keep busy, keep busy,* she thought, remembering that her new orders had arrived for the coming months. Glancing down at Captain Bonneville's list, she instantly felt better. She had told him that she wanted to fly to different airfields — deliver different planes — not just fly in and around London in S.E.5a's. And he hadn't disappointed.

The airfield at Biggin Hill required several Bristol fighters, Marham Aerodrome in Norfolk, Sopwith Pups for night flying, Old Sarum Airfield near Salisbury, five Airco D.H.4's, and there was also a delivery pending for two Avro 504's to R.A.F. Waddington, in Lincolnshire. Her cheeks dimpled at this — it meant a round trip of about two hundred and fifty miles. She had wanted to go further afield, and Lincolnshire was a step in the right direction. The challenge of delivering to different airfields would keep her sane, and flying planes she had flown in the past felt like reacquainting herself with old friends.

And then she turned the page. In late September, a batch delivery of S.E.5a's had been pencilled in for her. To London Colney Airfield.

One hundred miles away in northern France, Rick Randal had just returned from a lone dawn patrol. Landing carelessly, he threw his S.E.5a at a group of fir trees lining the airfield, the aircraft shuddering before taxiing haphazardly towards the huts and hangars. Swinging left, it narrowly avoided the squadron cook, who raised his fist, before finally coming to rest before their mascot, a wiry black Scottish terrier named Contact. Yelping, the animal relieved itself over a wheel at the same time as the pilot fell from the cockpit, skinning his leg in the process.

Flying at altitudes of up to seventeen thousand feet, Rick had felt sick, cold, and dangerously light-headed. The risks of oxygen deprivation were all too well-known, yet despite Ayda's suggestions and McCudden's results, there was simply no time for modifications. There was a war on, which had to be won.

Bloody April and Ludendorff's northern offensive had seen the R.F.C./R.A.F. decimated, over a thousand aircraft lost in five weeks. That hurt, as did the news that Richthofen's replacement, Ernst Udet, had just been saved by his parachute. So, whilst German pilots glided gracefully to safety, the R.A.F. pilots seethed watching them or else burnt to death in the cockpit of their planes. Trenchard's opinion, that parachutes would only encourage pilots to abandon their aircraft, still held. Consequently, none were offered. And that really hurt! *Maybe bloody Trenchard liked his pilots sizzling and burning while the Huns floated in the clouds?*

Rick consulted his wristwatch: 7:15 a.m. Thinking of parachutes, he vaguely recalled Ayda's ideas: fitting them inside the cockpit, under the seat, even stringing them to the aircraft's side, and afforded himself a scowl. A rumble reminded him of the returning dawn patrol: they would need debriefing, then formation flying drill and a tactics meeting, to be followed by more dive and zoom.

Someone tapped him on the shoulder, and he spun round.

'Second Lieutenant Boniface reporting for duty, sir,' a young voice squeaked.

Rick looked the youth up and down. 'So, you've come to help at 65a, have you Boniface? How many hours?'

'Twenty, sir.'

'Better than some. "C" Flight in forty-five minutes. Taff will take care of you.'

Captain Owen 'Taff' Davies, a stout Welshman, stepped forward, indicating for the young man to follow. Boniface remained stationary. Davies indicated again but Boniface merely cleared his throat.

'I would just like to say, sir, that I've read all about your antics and I much admire you, which is why I put in for 65a.'

An awkward hush followed. 'My antics — is that what they are? Well, I've a question for you, Boniface, before old Taff here whisks you away. Will it be sizzle, burn or fry?'

'I say, steady on, sir.' Captain Davies shuffled about awkwardly.

'Because that's what will happen without antics, my boy — probably with them, too.'

Rick knew he was being harsh, but he wasn't wrong. In the month of June 1918, pressure was mounting. An elite fighting squadron, equipped with the best scouts, 65a needed results fast, and as squadron commander he was responsible. Coinciding with this pressure, the calibre of newcomers arriving had dramatically declined. At first Rick kept up, setting up dives, easy targets for the less experienced, sharing his successes with bonhomie, increasing the squadron's score tenfold. But in the last few weeks, Rick had felt an eerie foreboding. An incessant restlessness made him work when he was meant to be sleeping, only then to collapse on his feet hours later. His obsession of jumping from a burning plane with no parachute began sapping the squadron's morale, so when the diagnosis came, it was a relief.

'Acute anxiety. Two to three weeks' rest.'

'That's too much, there's too much to do,' Rick protested. 'The squadron need me.'

The Medical Officer was blunt. 'They'll manage. Now off to Blighty with you.'

The man who appeared on Ayda's doorstep three days later was startling. Rick twitched, shook, tore out clumps of his sandy hair. His thin figure was hunched, the fierce look in his deep-set eyes his only recognisable feature. Yet slowly, during the fortnight he spent on leave, Rick became stronger again and he began to return to his old self.

'Take a stroll with me?' he asked Ayda, two weeks after returning, pointing at the winding path leading beyond the airfield. They had agreed to visit London Colney today for old times' sake.

She nodded and fell into step beside him.

'You know I'm going back on Friday?' He took her hand. 'I hoped we'd continue writing, but you've been distant these last few days. Have I done something wrong?'

Ayda shook her head, concentrating on the path. In the last fortnight, they had taken things very slowly, afraid of the depth of feeling they had for one another. She'd given him time, space to convalesce, and his recovery had been spent almost exclusively at the R.F.C. Club.

'I'm not sleeping well,' she said, 'that's all. I know I should be happy, and I've never felt happier seeing you again, you being here — but I feel guilty too — perhaps it's all too soon. I've been having some strange dreams…' She trailed off, and in her mind she saw Katia, her eyes imploring, dusky blue lips parted. And then there were the dreams of Adam as he smiled at her from a burning cockpit, the flames reaching greedily upwards to consume him, the residual smell of oil and burning flesh making her eyes and nostrils stream. But when she awoke with a start, they were dry, tearless as she huddled in her blanket, sweating yet chilled to the bone.

Rick passed a hand through his hair. 'What sort of dreams?'

'About people really,' Ayda replied. 'Everyone I've ever loved and lost. People I can never see or touch again. The dreams start off innocently enough then end in flames, and I think perhaps I'm being warned not to love you.'

Rick's head, now so close, didn't flinch. 'That's nothing new. Dreams of flames, burning — been having them for years. Show me a pilot who hasn't, Ayda? Even noncombat ones like you, everyone has them because we all take the same crazy risks every time we climb into a cockpit and shout "Contact". Will we come back down to earth, will we live to see another day, or will it all just end in flames?'

They had reached a small shed used to store all manner of equipment, from radio receivers and balloon canvas to flying goggles. Grey clouds hung low over the airfield, indicating a sudden change in the weather. And soon drops of rain the size of saucers descended from the darkened sky.

'I don't pretend to know all the answers, Ayda, but in the little time I may have left, I intend to live … and love.' Opening the shed door a fraction, a warm mustiness greeted them and, pushing it wider, he flicked on a light. 'After you,' he said, pulling her close, his hands around her waist.

The wind howled in, scattering a few dusty files, making the shed shake. Rick kicked the door closed — inside was warm, soft and safe — for now. Her green eyes met his deep blue ones. Laying down beside him, her breaths became uneven when his fingertips brushed lightly over her body, and she soon forgot about the storm outside.

CHAPTER 31

Ayda had heard rumours about the influenza sweeping through the country and she was anxious to make sure her mother was not ill. She had received a worrying letter from one of the nuns at St Catherine's saying her mother had been in an accident and she might want to visit. As she took the train to Ealing, it was clear that Londoners were scared, many wore masks covering their mouths, and she pulled her own scarf tightly around her mouth and nose, keeping her distance from the other passengers.

The convent was wreathed in a cold mist when she arrived. Inside the building, the same nun with the crooked teeth greeted her.

'Mrs Bound — so glad you could come.'

'How is she?'

'Comfortable. Your mother's gravely ill, but her memory seems to have improved and she has talked a lot about you over the last few days.'

'I wasn't aware my mother was speaking, at least, she wasn't the last time I visited. What happened to her?'

The elderly nun looked away. 'We put your mother in a room with no bars, as we hadn't realised she was a danger to herself. In the middle of the night she opened the window and fell, breaking both legs. The drop from her window was some forty feet. It seems she was in a state of confusion and thought the window was a door. We don't think she meant to harm herself.'

'Oh!'

'Mrs Bound, please be careful not to speak to anyone other than your mother. Some of our patients have come down with a terrible affliction, and our rooms are full, our nurses busy.'

Remembering the masks at the station, Ayda felt an icy chill on the back of her neck. People everywhere were falling ill, even some of the pilots and mechanics.

The nun read her thoughts. 'It is the deadly influenza. People are becoming sick, Mrs Bound,' she said, shaking her head. 'And quickly. We've seen it happen here. It's like they are drowning in their own body.' The nun made the sign of the cross.

'Drowning?'

'Yes, drowning in their own blood. We have never seen anything like it.'

Ayda felt a sudden urge to flee from the convent, but she could not leave without seeing her mother.

'It's all very quick. First, the patient turns blue, then a strange, rotting miasma fills the air — and finally they drown. Do be careful, Mrs Bound, and take this.' A white handkerchief was proffered.

Ayda quickly moved up the stone staircase, taking the steps two at a time.

At the top of the stairs a porter walked past, pushing a shrouded body. He tapped his mask as he passed by, and Ayda tied the handkerchief across her face.

As the door to her mother's room creaked open, ragged breathing filled the air. A small figure lay prostate upon a crate bed, the furthest end raised by a plank of wood. The sheet looked unblemished.

'*Ciao Mama, come stai?*'

Ayda drew up a chair. The change in Rosina was significant: she was gaunt, her short curls were coarse and suffused with grey. An eerie rattling emanated from Rosina's chest. She'd heard people speak of it, and knew it instantly. By mid-afternoon, all was quiet. A peaceful expression on her mother's face told Ayda she'd slipped away. Ayda noticed a small potted tree by the window, a rowan tree that had not been there at her last visit. Her mother, she knew, would approve, for it was said to ward off evil spirits, and help passage to the afterlife.

Outside, there was much activity. Rosina, she learned, had died from pneumonia brought on by breakage of both legs and her left hip bone. Her decline, she was assured, was quick and painless, and recalling the tortured breathing, she hoped this was true. A short burial service ensued along with the other casualties.

Unsurprisingly, St Catherine's was no stranger to funerals, but for Ayda, the service was both impersonal and deeply painful. The names of the departed was read out without emotion, the service more a chore than a celebration of life. After the blessing, she made her way to where Rosina had been interred, separate from the influenza graves. The earth looked fresh as she laid down a simple red rose. Her mother's favourite flower.

Finally, her head began to clear. Rick's last letter had said he was due a month's leave by the end of June. It was almost July now, and there was still no word from him. With broken limbs, death rattles and influenza on her mind, Ayda began to think the worst.

Across the Channel, Rick sat at the Calais dockside, watching huge waves crash against HMS *Loyalty*. *God knows how people sailed for a living*, he thought, smoking a cigarette, a sickness building in the pit of his stomach. If he vomited now, he might not be allowed on board, and he desperately needed this leave.

Again, his nerves were in shreds. If he couldn't escape this damned war for even a week, then he might as well just end it here and now.

The ship's funnel bellowed, jolting him from his dark thoughts. Time to board. Crowds rushed forward and were immediately herded up the gangplank and into the *Loyalty*'s grey interior: officers, cooks, prisoners, then the patients, first the walking injured, then the *lyers* — the stretcher cases, clutching their papers which gave them licence to proceed on board and move on with their miserable lives, but to where? Back home, wherever that was. And those who couldn't clutch anything had their papers pinned to them for all to see, addressed rather like parcels. Many were coughing and sneezing, despite the warm summer weather. If you weren't sick before you boarded HMS *Loyalty*, you probably would be when you disembarked, Rick mused. He swallowed hard. Why, oh why, couldn't they have found him a plane? None spare, the adjutant at St Omer had told him, and he tossed his cigarette over the side at the memory.

'Look, sir, I'm no mechanic,' Rick had said, 'but even I can see that the Pup and the S.E.5a have "O" ring trouble. Both are badly misfiring; surely they should be flown back to Blighty for modification?'

'Not a chance.' The adjutant shook his head. 'All buses are needed here. Orders is orders, sir.' And that was that.

The tremors started soon afterwards.

Rick lit another cigarette to calm himself. If they saw how bad he'd become, they'd probably send him to Craiglockhart asylum in Edinburgh instead of London. Such was his haste, he wasn't sure what address he'd put on his papers or where he should report to, so long as he had his Blighty ticket and was sent on his way. The funnel bellowed again, nausea almost overwhelming him.

Picking up his kit bag, a large shadow projected a beefy hand his way. Above the sea's growing roar, a voice boomed, 'Well blow me, if it ain't Major Randal.'

Rick stepped back, taking in the giant in front of him, and he was not short himself.

'Thought I recognised you from the newspaper,' the man said. 'Three in a day wasn't it, Major? Mighty fine to meet you, sir. I'm with the 103rd Aero Squadron. Used to be part of the Lafayette Escadrille before February. Heard of us boys, have you?' The man straightened his shoulders, maximising his six-foot-plus frame.

'I have,' Rick said with a nod.

'May I say what a mighty fine job you're doing, Major Randal, sir. Heard about all your jaunts, all sixty of them. That's a real impressive tally. Not quite up to old Billy's score, but mighty dandy all the same.'

Rick smiled. 'Yes, I suppose Major Bishop's score *is* unbelievable, isn't it?'

The man looked on good-naturedly. 'You boarding now? Mind if I join you?'

Before Rick could reply, the American grabbed their kit bags and headed towards the gangplank. 'Do I have much choice?' he murmured, the sea drowning his words.

Rick was not in the mood for company, but at least the chatty American would help pass the time. Luckily, his stomach held and before he knew it, he could see Blighty on the horizon.

CHAPTER 32

When Rick returned, he and Ayda decided to book a week away together. There was no denying the passion between them and they wanted to be together in private, away from prying eyes.

The Devon cottage was blissful: a river swept past an arched bridge yards from their door, birds sung in willow trees; and the lights of Lynmouth twinkled in the distance once night fell. Over that week, they rekindled their love for each other. Each day, they walked for miles and talked, trying to learn everything about one another. The previous night they had stayed up until dawn, discussing the war, the influenza pandemic, their future, if indeed there was one. Ayda told him about her father, and her hopes of finding him.

Rick looked at her. 'Are you sure he wants to be found? Why didn't he marry your mother; be a father to you?'

'I don't know.' Ayda looked away. 'But he's a good man. And a brave one too, I know it.' She had no proof, only a belief that inspired her.

'How would you know?' Rick said gently. 'He didn't stay long enough for you to remember him.'

'Would *you* go back home if it was dangerous — face the pack, stand up to the bullies like I know he did?'

'What do you think I do every time I step inside my S.E.5, Ayda?' Rick started shaking.

Her hand closed over his. 'The killings in Armenia. I heard about them from newspapers, what the Ottoman government did, but if I can believe in what *he* did — go back to Armenai, face that brutality, try to help, resist it — then it helps *me* live and be brave. It has given me confidence, pushed me on — so yes, I *have* to believe it, and in him.'

Rick's blue eyes looked doubtful, but his shaking lessened. 'Well, bravo, Ayda — for believing in something.'

Then conversation turned to the suffragette movement.

'Is there even any point in me having the vote?' Ayda said. 'It won't make a difference, things never change, and when women do get the vote, if things go wrong, then we'll get the blame too. So, as long as I can do what I enjoy, there's no need to care about politics — it's science and mathematics that interest me.'

Rick frowned. 'But I thought you were angry you couldn't attend scientific meetings, give a paper or contribute your findings?'

'That's to do with equality, and yes, men and women *are* equal, that's obvious, but I don't see how my vote would help. Whatever happens, I'd be choosing which man to vote for. They will never let a woman take charge.'

They sat in silence for a while and then fell asleep together, waking in the afternoon, before realising they might miss their three o'clock train.

Arriving late into Euston, they were walking towards the taxi rank when a newspaper caught Ayda's eye.

'Look at this!' Ayda cried, and Rick scanned the page.

V.C. AIR ACE KILLED IN FREAK ACCIDENT

Captain James Thomas Byford McCudden is believed to have crashed and died on taking off from Auxi-le-Château aerodrome in his S.E.5a aircraft on the evening of Tuesday 9th July.

Rick saw Ayda into a cab and promised to meet up with her later. He needed to find out what had happened.

An hour later at Audley House, a grim face greeted Ayda.

'Did you enjoy your holiday, Miss?' Bintie, her maid, was unusually tight-lipped.

'Yes, thank you, it was very relaxing.' Removing her gloves, Ayda sank into a chair. It felt good to be home. 'I wonder, Bintie, if Cook's still about, could she stretch to a light supper? It's been a long day with more bad news.'

Her maid remained put, frowning. 'Well, Miss, there's a problem. It's Cook, she don't want to work for you no more.'

Ayda took a deep breath. 'Would you care to explain?'

'Nothing to do with me, like, and I reckon Mrs Carruthers is entitled to her opinion.'

'Please, Bintie?'

Bintie relented. 'Mrs Carruthers has her standards — we all have, like, but she's a bit old fashioned.'

'Go on.'

'She's always had a soft spot for Master Adam like,' Bintie said, 'and she don't like how you've just moved Mr Randal in without a care, parading him under our noses. Mrs Carruthers won't see Master Adam replaced so easily.'

'As if I could.'

'Well, she thinks you have, and so do the rest of us. We've long memories Miss, and remember the young master growing up here. We won't forget him in a rush, even if you —'

'Thank you, Bintie, I appreciate your frankness. I will talk to the staff in the morning and please don't bother Mrs Carruthers, a pot of tea will suffice.'

Ayda settled herself in the armchair, awaiting Rick's return. He would have gone to the R.F.C. Club for news. He could stay there tomorrow — but not tonight. Her staff (she could never think of them as servants) would just have to put up with him until then.

Even now in the midst of trouble, Ayda looked upon Audley House as home, believing there was something deep within its foundations that made her feel safe. Perhaps because it reminded her of Adam? She let out a sigh. Life was difficult enough without going to war with your cook or your maid, but it couldn't be helped. Just then the door creaked open and a figure hovered in the doorway. It was a rather red-eyed Rick.

'I'd better not stay; I was lucky to gain entry.'

'Oh, don't mind them. Did you find out what happened?'

Ayda noticed that Rick's left leg was shaking.

'He was lost in heavy mist,' he explained. 'Thought he was at Boffles, found it empty, so decided to set off towards Auxi-le-Château. No one recognised him in his flying gear. Thought he was some newcomer, but they marked his map and sent him on his way.' He swallowed hard. 'It appears he took off into the wind and was doing a near vertical climb. At two hundred feet he did some sort of half roll turn, then just nose-dived straight into the woods. And he wasn't wearing his belt.'

'Was he stunting, Rick, showing off, do you think?'

'No, I don't think so, but no one knows for sure. Someone said his S.E.5a was misfiring, that the carburettors were wrongly installed, but that's hearsay. One thing is for sure, with the exception of you, no one knew an S.E.5a like he did. He was a mechanic long before he ever dreamt of flying. He could strip a bus with his eyes closed, so there's no way he'd have set foot in a defective crate.' Now Rick's hands were shaking and Ayda could only watch helpless as his nerves got the better of him. She stood and took his hands, gently caressing them, trying to soothe him.

'He was buried this morning at Wavans. All hush-hush. Very quick. Hardly anyone attended.'

'Goodness!'

'Seems the manner of his death wasn't heroic enough. Won a bloody V.C., but engine failure's an embarrassment. Not like that German bastard back in April with all the shebang from *our* side. Makes you wonder whose side the top brass are on!'

'Come to bed, Rick,' she took his arm and guided him towards the staircase. 'Nothing can be settled now. Engine's do fail. They can just stop working if they're pushed too hard. You've had a long and difficult day.'

Without another word they crept upstairs.

By 7 a.m. Ayda was in the front hall, addressing her staff. Rick had already left.

'Like you all, I loved my husband, your master, and miss him dreadfully. No one is replacing him, nor indeed could, for that matter. However, I have sought comfort with his best friend, Major Rick Randal, another flying man who knew him extremely well. Adam befriended Major Randal, trained him and loved him like a brother. I'm sorry if some of you find this distasteful, but please be heartened by the fact that, like you all, Major Randal had a very special place in his heart. I am, however, aware of your sensibilities, so have asked him not call at Audley House for the present time. I hope we can now put an end to this matter and look to the future.'

The final week of July 1918 brought some of the hottest weather that summer. Ayda planned to escape with Rick to the coast for a few days. Their week in Devon felt like a long time ago, and Audley House felt morose under her staff's watchful eyes. Freedom, a chance to relax and plan their future, was sorely needed.

After lunch, the morning papers arrived. Opening a window to dazzling sunshine, the heat in the drawing room seemed oppressive, and Ayda gulped for air. Her head ached and she had a sudden sense of foreboding. When Rick settled beside her, *Daily Mail* in hand, she was sure of bad news. Cradling her head, she sat waiting. It wasn't long in coming. The paper was scrunched into a ball, and tossed aside.

'Who now?' she asked.

'Mannock. Edward Mannock of 85 Squadron.'

'But how can that be, the man's indestructible?'

'Seems he went down not far from Pacault Wood, early yesterday,' Rick whispered. 'He was helping a young New Zealander — name of Inglis — to shoot down his first enemy plane. Ever the instructor, I can see it now: setting things up, baiting the helpless two-seater, making it nice and easy, giving the boy confidence. Typical Mannock. But what the hell was he doing following it down? Seen at 200 feet, maybe lower. Then he was hit by ground-fire and went down in flames over the German lines. They haven't recovered his body yet.'

'But wasn't he a great strategist?' Ayda tried to remember his famous mantra, but Rick was already repeating the words:

'Always above, seldom on the same level, never underneath. Never leave formation. And never, ever follow your prey all the way down.'

His three golden rules. And he'd broken every one of them.

'I don't understand it. What could he have been thinking of? And the flames, Ayda, his greatest fear. Let's pray he used his revolver.'

She shuddered, not knowing what to say. How could the highest scoring British ace have got it so wrong? Bad luck maybe, but she didn't think so. Another ace gone and she couldn't help thinking it might be Rick next.

The following day, Rick packed up early and left for the station alone. He hated goodbyes, refusing to utter the word in case it became a reality, but his mind was now troubled with conflicting orders: *Report to St Omer — re-join 65a — take charge of 85*. Mannock's old squadron.

On the train from Waterloo, two young second lieutenants were discussing the demise of the ace, and, burying himself in a corner seat, Rick covered his face with his cap.

'See another ace's copped it. Dropping like flies, they are.'

'Certainly are,' his friend agreed. 'July's been a bad month. How many hours you got?'

'Including my training, about twenty-five. What about you?'

In his seat, Rick shifted uneasily, desperate for sleep.

'Same. About as many as that Inglis who was with old Mannock. They haven't found him yet. Supposed to be up near Butter Lane somewhere but the co-ordinates don't match. Could really do with a Mannock where we're going.'

'Too right,' his friend replied. 'Not too many of them big aces left now. First McCudden, now Mannock. Who's next?'

'Well, you know what they say … things go in threes, don't they?'

At this, Rick stood up, placed his cap on his head, and left.

CHAPTER 33

'Feeling all right, sir?' the adjutant asked, looking into Rick's eyes.

'Never better! But I say, where the deuce is Vignacourt?' Rick grabbed a map, slurping tea from a tin mug as he plotted co-ordinates. Today he'd volunteered for something completely different, noise duty in an F.K.8.

'Noise duty?' he'd exclaimed when initially approached. 'That's a new one.' He knew the Armstrong Whitworth F.K.8's were noisy beasts — but noise duty?

'Low flying, sir,' the adjutant had explained. 'Over enemy trenches, the engines drown out approaching tanks. Noisy buggers, they are, those F.K.8's, just the ticket for spotting anti-tank batteries too.'

Rick stood a minute before opening his tent, imagining the thud-thudding of a low-flying F.K.8. Then a strong breeze whistled past him, sending his maps flying, making him turn around and look back inside. He could hear someone speaking

'I beg your pardon; can you speak up?' Rick asked, before poking his head out and looking around. There was no one about. But he'd heard something. *Strange*, he thought, fastening his jacket. Dragging himself across the grass to his waiting S.E.5, a mechanic gave the machine a once-over. His knuckles were bleeding, his fingers grazed. Like pilots, mechanics were working at full pelt, dealing with all the mishaps and breakages from A, B and C Flights' five daily outings. The S.E.5s were continually shot at, resulting in cracked fuel lines and bullet marks, their round-the-clock usage, often by inexperienced pilots, manifesting in damaged wingtips, splintered propeller blades, broken canvas from snapped strut wires, smashed spars, misfiring engines, carburettor trouble, and even lopsided undercarriages.

The patches on the wings jittered as Rick climbed in and shouted, 'Contact', just as the same voice he had heard a minute ago again whispered in his ear. He turned around, recognising it as belonging to Edward Mannock, but then he remembered he was dead. *Odd*, he thought, tapping his ear.

Taking off from Vignacourt just after dawn, he steered his S.E.5a towards the German lines. Despite a blanket of heavy mist, an F.K.8 had already set off. Flying closer to the lines, the familiar *ack-ack* of the anti-aircraft fire made him groan as he dodged the Archie fire. Looking off-side, he noticed a small hole in the mist from which seven blueish-tinged objects had emerged, all weaving like angry mosquitos. In the distance sat their target, the lone F.K.8 two-seater. Rick swallowed hard, his heart missing a few beats as he dived, trying to reach it. But his help wasn't needed. After several bursts of fire, he watched, awestruck, as the F.K.8 forced the enemy into a full retreat.

Back at Clairmarais, the squadron listened to the story of Captain Ferdinand 'Freddie' West scaring off the enemy in his cumbersome F.K.8. And then hours later, and tiring of the tale, Rick was greeted by a full moon and a sky streaked with red, like it had been dunked in blood.

Unusual, he thought, for a warm summer's evening, then the shutters started flapping and a stray silvery beam shot through his tent, accompanied again by a breeze. *I'll be off now to look at the stars, old man*, a familiar voice whispered, *pass me my charts, please.* The hair on the back of his neck prickled, and his skin got goosebumps. *Adam*? Knocking over an oil drum, Rick shot outside — but no one was there. Perhaps stress was catching up with him? They were all fighting harder than ever: five patrols a day, on and on, until who knows what? Something had to give.

Five weeks later, in early September, Rick awoke with a jolt at daybreak. His legs felt like lead, the remnants of a headache clinging to his neck; and the cloying air telling of another baking day ahead. Reclining onto his pillow, he gulped at the air, trying to wake himself. Music swept in through the tent: strains of *Danny Boy* sung in a descant with a violin accompaniment plucking slowly at the notes of the familiar *Londonderry Air*. The last time he'd heard it, the ace Edward Mannock had played it for him. Again, a breeze filled the tent and Rick shot out into the early dawn. The music stopped.

'What the dickens?'

The morning was silent. Back inside, the music started again, and Rick cradled his head, willing it to cease. Taking a deep breath, he crossed the airfield. Mechanics were preparing for the dawn patrol. In the mess, pilots moved in and out and he spotted who he was looking for, Lieutenant Albright, the gangly squadron musician.

'I say, Albright,' Rick said. 'A bit off practising your violin at this ungodly hour. Gave me a shock waking up to old *Danny Boy*.'

'I'm sorry, sir, but it wasn't me,' A delicate finger swept across Albright's forehead, where sweat was already gathering. 'Haven't been able to play a note since we lost Turner. Haven't had the heart for it.'

Rick studied the young man. 'Of course, Albright, you and Turner were very close.' He hoped he'd said the right thing. Still, he was angry. Why was Albright lying? It had to be him. Rick's left leg began to shake.

'I say, sir, here are our two replacement pilots.'

Rick swung round, almost colliding with the adjutant, who introduced the two fresh faces: Sowerby and Beecham. He managed a smile. 'Well, men, welcome to 65a. How many hours?'

The shorter of the two, Sowerby, inched forwards, swelling out a weedy chest. 'We've both got nine hours, sir.'

'Any manoeuvres, rolls, spins? Immelmanns ?' Rick asked.

'I watched somebody looping once, and I think I can bank all right,' Sowerby replied.

Rick pulled at a clump of sandy hair. 'Any firing practice or low flying?'

'Well, no, sir,' Sowerby admitted. 'We were told we'd get plenty when we reached France.'

'Good God, man, don't they realise there's a war on? What about you?' he pointed at Beecham. 'Ever flown an S.E.5?'

Beecham hesitated. 'I saw one once at training, but they said I was probably too large for it.' He flushed, looking at his feet.

'Well, there's nothing for it,' Rick said, sighing, 'we'll just have to squeeze you in. Now, listen hard, both of you. You're to stay at the very back of the formation behind Gordon, Peters and Albright. If an enemy plane comes near you, turn around and head for home. And for goodness' sake, keep out of trouble.'

Frowning, Sowerby folded his arms. 'I say, sir, with all due respect, aren't we going to take a pot at the Hun? I mean, that's what we signed up for. Not much fun otherwise!'

Rick strode over, grabbing him by his shiny new wings. 'I'd say you're about four years too late for the fun. And if you think being shot down in flames, crash landing because your engine's given up the ghost, jumping from your bus without a parachute because we haven't got them, or blowing your brains out with your revolver to avoid the other three, sounds like fun, then congratulations, you've come to the right place.' He gulped in some air before continuing. 'Seriously, you two, just remember: if your engine fails, don't try and turn around, just carry on, that way you'll crash land straight. If you do manage to take off, just follow me and do exactly what I do. Got that?'

Sowerby and Beecham nodded.

Later, Rick watched in horror as Sowerby bounced and skittered across the grass like a drunken tennis ball, pulling his nose up at the last minute to avoid a copse of trees. And once airborne, Beecham was incapable of maintaining his speed, almost colliding twice with Albright, zooming past his C.O. to the front before suddenly pulling back and losing height. Near St Bernard, this was repeated, attracting the attention of a two-seater Spad and its accompanying scouts. Within seconds, one scout had singled out Beecham, firing a volley of bullets into his canvas and narrowly missing his fuel tank.

Rick signalled to Albright before diving to the left and going after the attacking Albatros. The Albatros pilot stunted and looped for all he was worth but couldn't shake him off, and a sickening whine revealed he was in trouble.

At first, the plane carried on, then something bright flickered on its wingtip. Seconds later, black smoke billowed from the rear. Rick watched the pilot jump, parachute intact, before reaching for his revolver. Rick's shot was well-aimed. Wasting no time, he performed an *Immelmann* turn, arriving behind the Spad and the second scout. From the corner of his eye, he noted two things: Albright's machine was misfiring, and the formation was intact.

Rick signalled to Peters, who then swooped down on the two-seater. Rick re-loaded his Lewis gun and fired two bullets. One crashed through the skull of the observer, the other hitting the pilot between the eyes. Albright was still airborne, so Rick signalled for him to head home with the newcomers, and together with Peters and Gordon, he set off in pursuit of the third Albatros, who was sprinting towards the German lines.

Scanning the sky for more tell-tale grey-blue dots, Rick stuck hard to the scout, who met his fate over Lens. Two hours later, the report came from the artillery confirming the squadron's third kill of the day.

The next morning, Rick ran towards the hangars as the mechanics carried out their first checks for the ten o'clock patrol. He could hear the voices again and he was determined to find the source. On hearing their C.O. muttering to himself, the mechanics looked up.

Rick was repeating Albert Ball's words as they were whispered in his ear, no longer bothering to look around for the source or shake his ears as if to remove wax. '*Feel utterly rotten. Like I am becoming a murderer. Feel absolutely through, all in.*'

'Good morning, sir. Looks like it's another fine day,' Lieutenant Hepsworth, the oldest mechanic, said, getting Rick's attention.

He looked at the mechanic. 'Get my plane fuelled and ready.'

Without a word, the mechanics wheeled his machine out as he waited.

A month later at the start of October, after nearly two hundred patrols, Rick sat on his bed. The weather had turned: a thin frost covered the grass with horizontal sheets of rain teeming down. Drumming his fingers on an upturned oil drum, he glanced at the photograph of Ayda which sat on its top — there she stood, smiling in front of her S.E.5a, her hair streaming out in all directions. But he wasn't really looking or thinking of her. Not today.

A German pilot had crossed his path the evening before, mimicking his style, his turns. Everything was mirrored precisely by the enemy in his navy-blue triplane. Their paths had crossed close for an instant yet neither fired, though both could have, and with a slight inclination of his head the Fokker pilot had then dived towards the German lines. Who was he?

The canvas of Rick's hut began flapping as a cool breeze swept in. As usual, the breeze wasn't alone. Who did it bring now, he thought, as a soft voice whispered in his ear: '*His flying was wonderful, his courage magnificent and in my opinion, he is the bravest German airman who it has been my privilege to see fight.*'

The very words of his friend James McCudden, spoken this time last year after he'd seen Werner Voss's last flight. He was pleased McCudden hadn't forgotten him because he was lonely now, and he enjoyed hearing his friends speaking to him: Adam Bound, Edward Mannock, James McCudden. Even young Albert Ball had called upon him — killed at just twenty, and now forever young.

Perhaps he might meet the navy triplane again, things might be different if they weren't alone, then he might see his friends for real and talk to them properly. He dearly wanted to.

CHAPTER 34

Captain Bonneville's words danced before Ayda's eyes, and she re-read his note until she got to the line: *It might prove an adventure*, which made her smile. Her catalogue of missions to date had been sedate, repetitive. But this was different. Captain Bonneville had found a mission to occupy her, a round trip of over eight hundred miles taking her across a border, and though Scotland wasn't France, it was a start. Ayda would be delivering a brand new S.E.5a from Farnborough to the Number 1 School of Aerial Warfare at Ayr. Four days away, alone — in the air, in the sky — flying a trusted friend. Time to relax, stop thinking about Rick — and maybe there'd be a letter from him on her return?

When she arrived at the airfield the next day her S.E.5a sat on chalked grass spluttering with its surge of oil. Taxiing it around, she knew to expect the usual squeaking from over-tightened nuts and bolts or overstretched canvas, but there would be time to break in this shiny stallion. Lodging a small valise under the seat, she paused, noting the space next to it that could fit a parachute. After more than four years of war, their pilots were still waiting for parachutes. How many lives might have been saved if they'd had them?

Ayda checked for normal oil pressure as the machine warmed up at around one thousand revolutions, and with the stick hard back, the static revolutions rose to around two thousand. Selecting hot air, the S.E.5a engine noted the change — *good*, she thought, quickly toggling back to cold air. Still at normal oil pressure after dropping to 100 rpm, the new machine sat purring and poised.

Settled in her seat, stick forward, the S.E.5a started to move off, eventually climbing at a speed of eighty knots. Ayda looked around, still delighting in the rush of earth and sky. She checked the fuel, looking over the side as puffs of white clouded the scenery. The S.E.5a had an endurance of two and a half hours, including twenty minutes on the emergency tank. Easing back on the stick, she hoped it would get her to the refuelling point at Scale Hall.

Ayda knew little about the airfield except that it was located somewhere between Lancaster and Morecambe, with several swiftly erected portable structures called Bessonneau hangars on the field which were used for visiting aircraft. She had been told the only facilities there were tents for men only.

Changing behind the odd oil drum was one thing, but for four days? So it had been arranged that a tender would await her at Scale Hall, taking her the short distance to lodgings at Morecambe, where she would be more comfortable.

Ayda reflected on the loneliness of a dispatch pilot. Being the only female pilot was even more isolating. The men in France had their squadrons for company though some, like Rick, preferred the company of lone patrols. Rick… There he was in her thoughts yet again. And she had been doing so well up till now. Suddenly, the S.E.5a dipped its nose and hiccupped, letting her know it was still there, working hard for her at six thousand feet. She patted its hard cocoon and wing-tipped down to the left, to begin her descent. With the Pennines in the distance and minimal buffeting from the prevailing westerly, Ayda dropped to three thousand feet.

England's answer to the Eiffel Tower rose before her, like an iron giant watching over Blackpool Pier and Pleasure Beach —

except pleasure was in short supply. The sand around Blackpool Tower looked grey, crumbling into a murky sea, and the beach was deserted as she flew over it. Disappointed, she headed to her landing point, but Scale Hall Airfield did little to raise her spirits. It was indeed just a stopping point: unloved and overlooked. Fortunately, the tender was there waiting to whisk her away to her lodgings on Morecambe seafront.

A wave of exhaustion hit Ayda as she dragged herself up the stairs to her room at Seaside Lodge. On entering, she pulled the sash windows open and leant out, hoping the sea air might revive her. The seafront swept before her and a little boy and his dog ran after a crimson kite, but the rush of salty air failed to energize her. Perched on the bed, her head felt heavy and she decided to take a nap before dinner. Perhaps adventures didn't suit her, after all.

Shafts of gold poured in with the early morning breeze as Ayda sat upright, squinting at a clock on the wall. Six a.m. The tender would be here in an hour. She had meant to rise last night, take in the sights and walk on the beach, but instead she had just slept. Some adventure this was, she thought, heaving herself up and splashing her face in the basin.

She tucked into breakfast ten minutes later, and vacated the lodgings soon after, before boarding the tender.

Refuelled and ready, her S.E.5a was waiting. Up in the sky, heading north and slightly westwards, she checked compass, coordinates, oil pressure and speed. The weather ahead didn't look promising. After two hours, the border between the two countries nestled below, a continuation of the same piece of land and air, and Ayda was surprised there was no distinct demarcation — unlike the Channel between England and France.

The gloom increased, the wind direction suddenly changing to a forceful northerly which amplified the turbulence. Ayda could feel sidewinds buffeting her tail and wings, reducing the airflow. Soon raindrops spattered her windshield and goggles, and she tried not to stall, her eyes fixed on a blurry horizon. The rolling continued; she adjusted her tail, but the yaw of the S.E.5a kept changing. Beginning her final descent, the grass grew denser, greener, packed between cliffs and rolling golden sand dunes, and she noted the blue sea waving below.

Flying over Turnberry, her back stiffened. What greeted her was worse than turbulence or rain: a group of five or six mosquito-like machines swarmed in the distance, rising up, then yo-yoing down, somersaulting over each other. Heading her way.

Ayda dropped her speed and lowered the plane's nose, her hands sticking fast to the stick. Aiming to fly under the swarm, she froze, noticing tiny pinpricks of light flashing from each plane, a few even coming towards her. They were firing at each other! She rubbed her goggles. Was she meant to join in — engage with them? The S.E.5a shuddered in answer, and deciding against it, she soon spotted a chalky landing area. Within minutes, she had bumped to the ground and was wheeling safely on grass.

Climbing out, her legs wobbled and her fingers slipped as she held on to the sides of the plane. The machines and flashes of gunfire in practice had shaken her, unsettling her more than she could have imagined — and now she felt ashamed. How could she have ever wanted to fight in France? If this was what Adam and Rick had to put up with, she wanted none of it.

Removing her goggles, Ayda looked about the airfield, taking in its size. No one came to greet her. Gone was the fanfare, the clapping from curious onlookers that had marked her earlier career. Just as well. She couldn't face them now. Looking ahead, a massive sign dominated the landing area: NUMBER 1 SCHOOL OF AERIAL WARFARE.

She had got her wish at last. Adventure and aerial warfare. But she wasn't sure she liked it.

Removing her flying helmet, she rubbed her ears. The sound of guns firing was still around her. This was no play act, no rehearsal. This was war. And this was *the* place to learn how to shoot, how to kill in the air. Most of 65a had been through Ayr. Rick had been here, and so had James McCudden, instructing here just months before his death.

She found her lodgings in a tent away from the main mess building, behind the mechanics' hangars. Still, no one had met her, but she didn't care; at least someone had realised it was best to keep her separate. That suited her fine. After discovering there were facilities, she made her way to her guest tent, collapsing on the cot bed laid out for her, thinking it was the same as those described by Adam and Rick. All part of the adventure, she supposed, struggling to remove her flying boots.

The next morning, the tent was bathed in a crimson glow. Here, there was no wall clock but from the sun's position, Ayda judged it was around 6 a.m. Time to move, except that her body didn't feel inclined to do so. She knew she had experienced this level of lethargy before, but felt too tired to remember when, how or why. Noisy activity outside got her to her feet, and then she looked down, her cheeks flaming in shame — she had slept in her flying clothes.

In less than an hour, she was standing by the S.E.5a for exchange, listening to the observations of its chief mechanic.

'Aye, it's a bit shot to pieces. Look here,' he said, shaking his head and pointing to the upper wing. 'Three wee shells all lodged around that strut.'

Remembering yesterday's welcome, Ayda's face was a picture and the mechanic grinned at her, showing a set of gappy teeth. 'You didnae know they were blanks?'

'Yes. Of course — naturally — I did,' Ayda squeaked, the tips of her ears burning in her flying helmet. 'Still, I'd like to do my own checks, if that's okay?' Removing a spanner from her valise, now it was the mechanic's turn to gape.

This 'new' S.E.5a wasn't new by any stretch, only a much-shot-at workhorse badly in need of a rest. Glancing at the patched wings, she opened the engine canopy and peeked inside. Having seen what the so-called elite pilots at the Central Flying School could do, she wasn't surprised at the damage.

Finishing the work an hour later, she began readying herself for the return journey. Although this was meant to be an adventure, she had no desire to return in a deathtrap. But at least she *had* a choice. The men in France didn't. They flew what they were given. Feeling emotional, she patted the lower wing. This S.E.5a would be feeling much better now — even if she wasn't.

Ayda's four-hundred-mile return journey was much like the outward one, only in reverse, and she got to walk along the beach at Morecambe this time. When she returned to Audley House, a pile of letters was waiting for her. Thumbing through them, she sat down in an armchair with an aching head and tingling fingertips. There was no word from Rick.

CHAPTER 35

A few weeks later, Ayda circled the Shenley airfield, masses of green cornfields in miniature were in her ring sight. She wing-tipped to the left, beginning her descent as if in a trance, and the next thing she knew, she had taxied to a standstill, feeling as if the S.E.5a had landed itself. London Colney had that same state of readiness about it, still funnelling all the elite through on their way to the front, making sure they were tiptop and ready for war. But an unmistakeable air of tiredness hung about the place. The buildings, the huts and hangars constructed less than two years before, had begun to look dishevelled.

Ayda looked around knowingly. The airfield was war-weary like everything — and everyone — else. Paint had scraped off the woodwork, the fields had grown unruly around the main take-off area and landing points, and pieces of canvas lay about, muddied with grease and aviation fumes. Oil drums were left rusting on their sides, while some of the canvas huts were covered in grime along split and fraying edges.

To most, London Colney was still a shining example of aviation superiority, but Ayda knew better. It looked tired as if, like her, it had had its fill. Two figures caught her eye: one stocky with dark curly hair, the other tall and thin with sandy hair, but when she turned again, they were gone. Ghosts perhaps, she thought, feeling sick — but of whom? Two names whispered in her ear: *Albert Ball and Rick Randal.* Both had flown from here, and she was increasingly unsure whether or not Rick would ever return.

The following day, back at home, she sat at her drawing room window, waiting. She'd dressed carelessly that morning as had become her habit: a functional tweed skirt over a delicate silk blouse crushed by a heavy belted cardigan. Perhaps there'd be a letter today? In the beginning, she'd received one a week from Rick, but now she had to contact people in the R.A.F. to check that he was still alive. Rick's last note hadn't made sense. It had spoken of imaginary 'castles in the air' inhabited only by the best pilots, or the 'kings of their game', as he'd put it. But there was no game.

Glancing at her letter pile, Ayda had never felt so alone. Others had been lost too: friends, acquaintances and several of the aces, but what if Rick was to die? She could take any hardship or inconvenience — but not that. Her feelings for him were real, beyond regard, admiration or deep friendship. It was love.

She opened a letter from Captain Bonneville at Farnborough.

30th September 1918

Dearest Ayda,

How are you? Hoping you enjoyed Ayr. I am yet to receive your report but am wiring your October orders anyway, certain they will cross. Very busy here; my leg has been troubling me and may not be connected for much longer. As one-legged airmen are not the rage, I'm to be moved permanently back to pilot training at Gosport. Recently, I've been on a sabbatical at Farnborough helping them out as they are so desperately short of ground pilots. I am afraid it isn't very exciting but chances are that you will be donning your very fetching flying gear here again soon. I wouldn't ask if things were not at breaking point, naturally your oily friends have missed you.

Contact and away, my dear, Captain Bonneville

Such a kind man, Ayda thought, picturing Captain Bonneville, remembering his bear-like hug. He'd served her well over the last two years, discretely arranging her flying work, making sure she flew the newest planes — but he would be disappointed. She could no longer face flying until she knew Rick was safe. She wasn't feeling herself: still exhausted, her nights were punctuated with vivid dreams, a raging thirst and a strange metallic taste in her mouth. Influenza was proliferating across the country in a second more deadly wave, and three of her household staff were nursing relatives at home. She hoped she wasn't succumbing.

Across the Channel at Clairmarais South aerodrome, Major Rick Randal awoke, feeling calmer and more rested than he had done for months. He'd slept well with no disturbances, and his head felt clearer too. The day was also fine. The early morning frost was melting in the sunshine, and the smell of fried bacon and toast wafted in from the mess tent, making his stomach rumble.

Stretching his long legs and reaching over to the upturned oil drum, he examined Ayda's picture — how beautiful she was! Bringing it closer, he studied her features, trying to remember her in detail. A faint scent of lavender permeated his nostrils, and he clutched the picture. What would she be doing now, he wondered, as he settled down to pen her a letter.

An hour later, he emerged in the mid-morning sunshine, greeted by an almost cloudless sky. High overhead a gold and pink trail swirled, the sun creeping out from behind thin clouds as if playing hide and seek.

'Snow is forecast later,' the adjutant informed him.

'Already? That's early.'

'That's what they're saying. Better get your flying done, sir. Which patrol are you on today?'

'I was thinking of going straight up,' he replied, ignoring the question.

'Don't think your bus is quite ready yet, sir,' but Rick was already walking away. Soon, he was nearing the hangars where a sheepish young mechanic greeted him.

'Lovely morning, Farthing,' Rick said. 'You haven't by any chance seen my bus, have you? Funny thing, but it appears to have gone AWOL.'

'Afraid, sir, it's all in pieces,' the mechanic replied slowly. 'Having a complete overhaul, sir. Fitting new spars and an undercarriage to it, like. Might be ready this evening but you best check with Lieutenant Hepsworth when he's back from the latrines.'

'Thank you, Farthing. Any planes spare?'

The mechanic looked towards the latrines. 'No, sir, only 'Ghost', but no one wants it on account of what happened to Beecham.'

Rick swallowed hard. Beecham's propeller shaft had come loose as he was landing, and severed his head. The plane had landed perfectly. Best landing he ever did was the joke around the airfield, or that the plane had somehow landed itself. Subsequently the mechanics had nicknamed it 'Ghost', and the name had stuck.

'Fuel her up and get her started,' Rick said, putting on his helmet.

Farthing smiled weakly and set to work.

At twelve thousand feet the air thinned rapidly. Rick felt the familiar light-headedness and the numbness in his extremities. He was glad to be on lone patrol; formations were risky with all the new pilots coming out of Blighty, most of whom could barely fly.

He ascended another few thousand feet and, scanning the horizon, decided to head northwest towards Fricourt. After all, he did have a full tank of fuel.

And then something joined him from behind the sun: in his mirror he spied a dark dot speeding towards his tail.

The safest option would be to change direction and make for the Allied lines, or run for home. Instead, he side-winged right, turning his S.E.5a to face the navy Fokker D.VII, and saw to his horror eight more navy dots emerging from behind the sun. Barely visible and strewn above the horizon, they were hurtling towards him at great speed.

Licking his lips as he dodged the bullets from the Fokker, he twisted and turned, and side-slipped out of its way. Catching a glimpse of the pilot he realised with a shock that it was the same man he'd engaged with the day before, and now the Jasta formation was almost on him.

With no time to think, he grabbed his revolver and fired directly at the lead Fokker's wingtips. It hiccupped, lost height, then steadied and rushed at him again with three other triplanes right on his tail. It was time to find out whose nerves could hold the longest.

Rick lowered his head, kicked his rudder bar, and manoeuvred his S.E.5a so it was heading straight at the leader. He released more bullets even as the lead triplane continued on its course towards him, until — with about thirty feet to spare — the pilot lost his nerve, pulling his nose up in the nick of time. Rick smiled at this small victory, then heard an unnatural, deafening noise behind him: a clanking, whooshing sound he'd never heard before, and he'd flown at one hundred and twenty miles per hour many a time.

The joystick became rubbery and unresponsive.

He grabbed it hard, swinging it forwards then backwards in an attempt to regain control.

Despite his efforts, the plane started sliding backwards and down, and from the corner of his eye Rick saw the looming dark, navy shape coming at him again. He needed to put his plane into a tailspin if he was going to get out of this — never his manoeuvre of choice unless absolutely necessary, as it was now. He spiralled his plane towards the earth, but to his surprise found he wasn't alone… The Fokker was following him down.

Affording himself another smile, he heard a whisper in his ear: *Never, ever follow your prey all the way down.*

He grabbed his revolver, firing blindly at the triplane — he hit well, huge black plumes engulfing it. But his own cockpit was becoming hotter now, and the earth loomed ever closer. The heat was searing, and thick, acrid smoke billowed outwards, making his eyes stream.

There was only one option.

His hands shook as he lifted the revolver.

He thought of Ayda.

I'm sorry. So sorry.

He thought of his friends already departed for their castles in the air.

The Fokker exploded below him.

He closed his eyes, lifted the barrel against his temple, and fired.

CHAPTER 36

On 9th November 1918, Kaiser Wilhelm II abdicated and Germany was declared a republic. News from the front came thick and fast, and an expectant air hung over London. Still there was no letter from Rick.

Ayda was restless. Flitting from room to room, a glance at her hallway clock confirmed it was 4 p.m. The dizzy optimism seized upon by many was driving her frantic until she could concentrate no more — the evening papers would be out soon, and she fancied some fresh air. Bintie often brought them up after dinner but today she couldn't wait. So, donning an elaborate hat of silk red roses and cream feathers and a new overcoat, she set off into the crisp afternoon air.

Crossing over to a nearby park, she could hear the cries from newsvendors.

'War stalemate continues,' a man shouted.

'Groener replaces Ludendorff,' another grunted, and then a much younger voice, 'Decorated ace falls.'

The headline was uttered quietly, and Ayda wasn't even sure she had heard it properly. Fear gnawed at her as she crossed the park towards the stand and its stack of papers. The boy repeated his headline, half smiling, pleased with the attention, unaware her world was unravelling fast.

With trembling fingers she handed him a coin. 'Which page for your story?'

'Page nine, Miss.'

Whether it was the biting cold, or her shaking hands, the pages stuck fast and would not open. Silently mouthing the words, *please, not him*, she eventually arrived at page nine. Now the printed lines clumped together in a dark mass as she looked for something recognisable, and, not seeing anything, she focussed again, hopeful now.

Then she saw his name.

A tiny entry in the bottom left corner of the page read: *Popular Pilot Major Rick Randal killed, 3rd October 1918.*

It was so small it was hardly there. She looked a second time, then a third, noticing a wave of weariness and nausea wash over her.

The street around her began to spin. The newspaper pile drew closer, and she felt she should look for a place to land, but why was she landing on newspapers? She heard a loud thud, thinking her wheels must have touched down…

But there was no aeroplane.

Ignoring the concerned faces peering down at her, Ayda picked herself up from the floor and drifted home in a daze. Once there, she locked her bedchamber door, and threw away the key.

Two days later, Ayda woke to the sound of gunfire. She stumbled to her bedroom window and saw a lone lorry lumbering down the street, firing anti-aircraft guns. Since learning of Rick's death, she'd requested her meals be left outside her door and she hadn't seen anyone, but she supposed if an air raid was imminent, then she would have to leave the house. Or would she? Either way, she didn't much care.

More sounds disturbed her. Noises of people — lots of people. Something uncommon was happening. A repeated booming sound from the Thames made her look at the horizon, then she realised what it was: all the boats, even the tugs, were playing a tune on their funnels. Next the church bells started. All across London the bells rang and then Bintie was banging on her bedroom door, shouting to be let in.

'Miss, oh Miss. Please open up… Please, Miss!'

Ayda looked at the door. The thumping was getting louder, the pleas more desperate. Still not dressed, she crept over, just as her maid opened it up with a spare key.

'Miss, oh Miss,' Bintie cried, grabbing Ayda around the waist. 'Isn't it wonderful news?'

Ayda didn't answer but remained fixed to the spot.

'I think it's all over, Miss. Isn't that splendid?'

'What's all over?'

'The war, Miss, or at least it will be at eleven o'clock.'

Ayda blinked at Bintie, not processing the information. Over? She had waited through the years, lain in bed dreaming about hearing these words, but they never came — until now. Too late. Raising her face to her maid, wondering why she was still talking, Ayda tried hard to listen.

'Please say something, Miss. Everyone's going outside to celebrate. They say Mr Lloyd George will address the crowds soon.' Bintie grabbed Ayda's cold hands, trying to shake some feeling into them.

Just then an omnibus clattered past. People were crowded onto the top deck singing, dancing, a few women even bashing trays and metal jugs with spoons and other items of cutlery. More buses passed with people spilling out over the top, all cheering and waving banners and Union Jacks.

'Say you'll come, Miss? Here, let me dress you. Put something warm on, it's chilly outside. Please?'

The pleading continued until Ayda was dressed in a staid woollen two-piece.

Once outside, the noise was deafening, the crowds overwhelming and before long, she felt herself carried along the street, swept on a tidal wave of humanity with people of all shapes and sizes, young and old alike, bobbing up and down, waving, dancing, cheering and shouting for all they were worth.

Ayda was carried along with the flow of people until they stopped at a half empty omnibus. People were climbing aboard, clambering up the stairs and she was pushed up. The buses had converted themselves into musical grandstands for the show fast developing. Nobody paid any fares because nobody asked for any. A large lady in a black high-necked blouse and matching skirt stood at the top deck, waving a banner which read, 'Kaiser go to Hell', and other banners were just as explicit.

As the omnibus crawled along to Downing Street, it passed cheering office workers hanging from windows with banners and flags draped down the brickwork. Then the munitions workers joined in, dancing a conga down the Strand with flags draped over their yellow-tinged skin. Wounded soldiers followed to Whitehall in their hospital blues.

The crowds didn't have long to wait. At Downing Street, Ayda strained her head round a tall bowler-hatted gentleman to view the doorstep of Number 10, where a man in a bow tie, with a bushy moustache and white swept-back hair, stood fidgeting as he prepared to address the crowds.

Now everyone was saying *hush*, *hush* and finally, the noise deadened and a silent lull hung above the crowds. The man on the steps then turned, and there he was — the Prime Minister, Mr Lloyd George, sweating despite the cold and grinning broadly from ear to ear. He raised his hands as the maroons boomed loudly. As they finished, he stepped forward, his blue eyes twinkling

He cleared his throat. 'I am glad to tell you that the war will be over at eleven o'clock today.'

The crowd erupted in cheers.

'You are well entitled to rejoice,' Lloyd George continued. 'The people of this country and our allies, the people of the Dominions and of India, have won a great victory for humanity. The sons and daughters of the people have done it! They have won this hour of gladness, and the whole country has done its duty. It has achieved a triumphant victory which the world has never seen before. Let us thank God.'

A few minutes later, Big Ben sounded the hour and the crowd went wild. Ayda was secreted off the bus and into the street by Bintie. She felt faint and sick. She wondered when she had last eaten and her throat felt as dry as tinder. Her nausea returned with a vengeance, and she turned to Bintie.

'I don't feel too good.'

She rubbed her eyes, feeling her legs go beneath her. Someone tried to catch her. This time, her landing was cushioned and she felt someone loosening her buttons, feeling her head, her pulse. She heard the word *doctor*. People were looking down at her.

Then she heard the words she had already suspected: *This woman is pregnant.*

But she couldn't feel any joy at the news. What did it matter if the war was over, if she had lost everyone who had ever mattered to her?

PART 4

CHAPTER 37

Four months after the war officially ended, Ayda gave birth to Rick's son, Carl Adam Richard Randal. She didn't return to flying. When Carl was one, she took a post at *Nature* magazine, recommended by former schoolmaster, Cameron Muir, who also worked there. Somehow, their relationship seemed destined to continue much as before: he assuming the role of mentor and she, as always, the pupil. With an overinflated opinion of himself, Mr Muir was, she reflected, one of the few people to remain untouched by the war.

'Can't get the staff,' he complained. 'Surprising, really, with all these so-called heroes everywhere. Do well to remember who kept Blighty going while they were off chasing glory and playing soldiers — there they sit, sneering, thinking *we* owe them something. I nearly tripped over one the other day, and the look he gave me — well!'

Ayda turned her face away in anger. Many returning soldiers were still out of work, and Ayda felt a great sympathy for them. Some had been reduced to begging on the street, particularly those badly wounded and unable to find a job to pay their rent. Life had treated her generation shabbily, she thought, often wondering how Adam and Rick would have fared if they'd survived.

Mr Muir caught her expression. 'Before you give me another of your looks, I should point out I was very fair — interviewed heaps of them — not a scientific bone in any of them. Of course, I knew straight away who'd be right for the position: someone analytical with a good scientific background and a first-class mathematical brain, someone who could actually read my writing too — there could only ever be one candidate.'

At least her contact with Mr Muir was limited. She was allowed to work from home with the occasional telephone call or visit to London to submit and collect work, which meant she could spend as much time as possible with Carl. After the trauma of Katia's death, Ayda had watched him like a hawk, marvelling at his health and his development. His only issue had been with one of his eyes; his left seemed to have a mind of its own. She had visited a consultant at the Royal London Ophthalmic Hospital, who had told her there was a slim chance of correcting it, but using spectacles whilst reading could help.

Once Carl was fitted out with spectacles, she found her local library and from the moment they were inside, Carl was entranced: curling up next to her as she read to him. Soon they were seasoned library members, and she was glad she had made the effort to read to him, whatever the outcome for his sight.

A few months later, in the autumn of 1920, Ayda had a sudden desire to visit France. She wanted to find Rick's grave, for Carl to see where his father was buried. People expressed surprise when they discovered their trip was to be by sea, not air, none appreciating it was how both Adam and Rick had perished. In the air, you were exposed, often with no escape — sometimes with only flames for company. So, all the mines and U-boats still left in the Channel wouldn't persuade her against sailing the sea.

'Thought you'd be first to try the new Imperial Airways W.8b,' Cameron Muir said, raising an eyebrow. 'Good, solid Rolls-Royce Eagle engines. Typical of you to do things the wrong way round — aeroplanes are so much safer now and you turn your back on them. Very odd, I must say.'

Pursing her lips, Ayda looked away. Despite reading articles on these new, safe, modern engines, she knew what happened when things went wrong, and, as well as losing the men in her life, she had also lost her nerve. Yes, she *had* loved flying, had craved it above anything else, but she'd also experienced a different side to it, and no amount of modern technology would ever change that.

The following summer, Ayda finally had everything booked and prepared for the trip. Journeying past the town of Albert in the Somme region of northern France, Ayda stared out of the train's window, shocked at the state of the flattened, pulverised landscape. She had built up a fairy tale image of France from descriptions she had heard, but before her eyes lay the price war had exacted. Everything was grey, pockmarked and utterly devoid of life. Ayda watched farmers bent low, toiling, trying to coax their damaged earth back to life, and she felt sadness for their loss. Most moving of all were the fields of red: poppies swaying on slender stems, telling their own stories of loss that brought tears to her eyes. She had heard people talk of them, but hadn't expected the effect it would have on her. Ayda decided she could look no more.

Carl had been watching her, clinging to a little metal toy soldier. 'Mama,' he said, bringing her attention back to him.

Forcing a smile, she thanked God for her son, not knowing how she would have stayed alive without him. 'Book,' he demanded, and she read to him for the rest of the journey.

After disembarking at Arras, Ayda and Carl headed towards the Fauborg d'Amiens Cemetery, the place to lay a wreath for a loved one whose body had never been found. She knew many a pilot's widow had made the same pilgrimage.

Ayda's gaze was lost upon a sea of white crosses, stretching out in every direction beyond the entrance, row upon row upon row. She thought about Adam and Rick, tears welling at the sheer scale of the graveyard.

She walked with Carl in her arms towards the rows. She had been given instructions as to where she would find Rick's burial place and she searched for Grave 10, Row E. Five airmen were marked at this spot, buried together. Rick was amongst them.

Ayda bent over the small white cross, clutching a single red rose. The breeze whispered past her, and, standing there in France, Rick's face seemed close, a faint scent of spice warming her skin as if his smell were all around her. She stood there remembering: his deep blue eyes, his soft voice, how being in love had overwhelmed her, and she ached for him now.

But Rick had gone. She showed Carl the grave and tried to explain to him the significance, but Carl was becoming restless. He was too young. At least she could tell him they had visited when he was older.

They'd done what she had intended. Her life before the war ended was over, there would be no going back. And she would never return here again.

Before returning home, Ayda took Carl east to the beaches of northern France, to a place called La Maye in the Baie de Somme. Racing between the waves, Carl's chubby legs splashed in the water, sending a skein of spray up to his sandy-blond ringlets. Ayda watched her son carefully, removing his spectacles, and wiping seasalt from them. A seagull flew low, scanning the beach for a target, and Carl waddled after it, dragging his mother along too. Cockle in beak, the bird flew up, skimming the water's surface before turning its head and uttering a mocking squawk at them.

The afternoon passed lazily: drinking lemonade, eating the picnic Ayda had brought with them, and even building a few sandcastles. Watching the sea wash them away, she closed her eyes, thinking of Rick's castles in the air. The cool water lapped at her feet, the sea gently whispering in waves, soothing her anger and pain.

Very few things felt right that year, but her trip was one of them. The time spent away was an opportunity for Ayda to work out what was important in her life and to lay the ghosts of the past to rest. She had also come to a decision. Since finding out the truth about her father, she had always planned to search for him, but after seeing how war had left France, a trip to the war-torn Armenian-Turkish border felt unrealistic.

Besides, she had no idea where to start looking. Perhaps Adnan Gulzar had already perished through his stance against the Ottoman government. The Young Turks, she knew, had created killing squads and their atrocities continued. And then there was the war the world had just come through.

Ayda closed her eyes, wondering if her father's reasons for abandoning Rosina so long ago even mattered amidst this bloodshed. She decided she would keep looking, but she wouldn't let it consume her. She needed to look to the future. She'd silently promised Rick at this graveside to love their son enough for the both of them, and she was determined to show Carl enough love to compensate for everyone else who should have been in his life.

CHAPTER 38

The following summer, Ayda was walking home from the offices of *Nature* magazine when someone called her name.

'Ayda, is that you?'

Ayda spun on her heels and bumped into a hard-handled object. A beautiful black and silver pram shone in the sunlight, its wheels squeaking to a halt. Ayda's eyes widened at the lady at its helm. 'Mabel? From Miss Brace's?'

The smile broadened. 'The very same one — I knew it was you. How are you, Ayda? And how was your war?'

Ayda could feel tears threatening at the question. Quickly, she buried her head inside the pram. 'Boy or girl, Mabel?'

'Boy,' Mabel said proudly. 'Takes just after his father too, bless him.'

Ayda could feel the tears about to spill over. 'I can see you've got your hands full, Mabel, so I'd better…'

Mabel laid a hand on hers. 'Stay. Please? I could do with some company. I was meant to be meeting my husband, you see, but he's been called away to an important meeting. Come for a cup of tea with me?'

Ayda nodded and composed herself, and they walked to a small café near the British Library. An enticing smell of roasted coffee made it seem the perfect place to stop, and Mabel peered in at her sleeping infant, before collapsing into the nearest chair.

'Those war years were tough, weren't they?' Mabel said, looking at Ayda. 'I lost my first husband at Ypres. We were only married a few months.' She dabbed at her eyes with a serviette then patted her belly. 'But if he had come back, I wouldn't have met my dear Cyril. He found me crying my eyes just out over there.' She pointed to a nearby bench. 'Offered me his handkerchief, he did. True gentleman he is, my Cyril And if I hadn't met him then I might never have had these two — well, almost two.' She patted her belly again. 'Cyril said we'd better get on with it because you never know what's round the corner.'

Ayda nodded, thinking how right Cyril was, while Mabel continued. 'Cyril's much older than me — more than twenty years, but it doesn't bother me. He's a great father and provider, and kind too.' She paused. 'What about you, Ayda? You've not really said much, but you've gone awfully pale.'

Ayda felt her throat constrict. The tears were building again, and she tried to find the right words but they kept sticking in her mouth: that her son would never know his father, that she'd lost a daughter — and almost everybody she'd ever loved.

A warm hand covered her own, gently squeezing it.

'Look, Ayda, I'm so sorry. No need to say any more. But how's about coming to my house? Our flat's only five minutes away. Very close to Cyril's job at the Foreign Office, and I can see you're in need a friend.'

Ayda began to feel better, but she had Carl to pick up. 'That's very kind of you, Mabel, but today I have my little boy to pick up.'

'You have a little boy? Why don't you bring him? He can play with my John. What about tomorrow or next week? I really meant what I said about helping.'

Ayda smiled. 'How about next Thursday?'

The following Thursday, Ayda arrived at Mabel's flat, carrying Carl.

'Oh my—what a poppet!' Mabel said as she welcomed them in. 'And look at all that hair! Though it doesn't look anyway as dark as yours, Ayda, so, he must take after his father.'

'You are quite right. He *is* the image of his father.'

Mabel patted her hand. 'Who'd have thought it, eh? The two of us, mothers to such handsome little boys. We'd never have dreamed it back then, plonking away on our typewriters like our lives depended on it, that old rottweiler patrolling up and down the aisles. And look at us now, both proud as punch. We've done well for ourselves, haven't we?'

Mabel was easy company, not judgemental or demanding, and Ayda confided in her about Adam and Katia, and Rick. Again, Mabel's hand found hers, and Ayda continued to feel better. She felt close enough to Mabel to ask a personal question.

'Mabel, can I ask a favour of you? You did say if you could help in any way, you would?'

Mabel nodded. 'Of course.'

'I'm not sure if I ever told you, but I never knew my own father. The truth of the matter is that I found out about him quite by accident. My mother had hidden him from me but I found his name on my birthday certificate.'

'Gosh.'

Ayda swallowed hard. 'So when Carl's father died, I realised we were both truly alone, unless of course, my father was somehow still alive. And I think I owe it to Carl to see if there is a family out there. Somewhere.'

'I see.'

'But there is a problem. My father lives in Armenia. Or at least that's where he was headed to before the turn of the century. And he could be elsewhere or even dead from the war or even from several other wars. And I thought… Well, I thought perhaps that Cyril might be able to help — you did say he worked in the Foreign Office, didn't you?'

Ayda swallowed hard again, her green eyes looking directly at Mabel's blue, wishing again that she wasn't always surrounded by so much death.

Mabel was staring hard at her before finally speaking. 'I'm sure we can do something — what's your father's name?'

'Adnan Gulzar.'

'Gulzar — yes, of course. And what did he do?'

Ayda balled her fists. 'Well, that's the thing, Mabel. I've really no idea. My mother's account of him was always very patchy. I have my birth certificate, and a letter I've written to him in both English and Italian because I couldn't quite stetch to Turkish or Armenian.'

Mabel nodded. 'Send me copies of those and I'll see what Cyril can do.'

A week later a letter arrived from the Foreign Office signed by Mr Cyril Baker, Chief Clerk, Under Secretary of State.

22nd June 1922

Dear Mrs Bound,

I thank you for your enquiry regarding the whereabouts of your father, Mr Adnan Gulzar. After the war, there has been much change and re-structuring here as we dismantle war time departments in order to determine the size and shape of a peacetime Foreign Office given the immense changes to the international situation.

As I am sure you will appreciate, a search of this nature can take time and may involve a 'paper-trail' of countries. Even so, focussing just on the country of Armenia with its peacetime population in excess of a million citizens, the task is gargantuan, and it is my opinion, that success would be unlikely, given that you have supplied no address, nor details of occupation, next of kin nor indeed any information to suggest that Mr Gulzar may still be alive. Please bear in mind too that record keeping across the globe varies considerably with the standard in Armenia incomparable to what we enjoy here in Great Britain.

Nevertheless, as a promise, to my darling wife, I will begin my investigations.

Your most humble servant,
Reginald Cyril Baker

Five months later, a bulky, battered manila envelope marked Foreign Office arrived. The letter inside was handwritten in both Italian and English, with lavish looped letters in blue ink. Laying it on her trembling knees, nausea and curiosity competed with each other.

My dearest darling Ayda,

Your letter has made an old man so happy. Many times over the years, I have wondered about you, where you lived, what you did, what you looked like? — even I regret to say, if you were even alive. Your mother was right to take you to England for a fresh start. The land of your father has many troubles, and I rejoice that you have been spared them.

Please believe me when I say I tried to find you, returning to Pollenza the following year. But there was no trace of you or your mother. Know that you were loved, and wanted and that if not for war, you would be by my side.

I have risen high in my country's Diplomatic Service which I believe is the only way to create policy for a safer world and future, to not repeat the mistakes made this century.

And no, you are not alone, Ayda, you have two sisters and four brothers. I enclose a photograph of myself and your brothers and sisters who wish you to write to them, as do I. Perhaps we can one day meet in person?

With much love,

Your father

The picture swam before her eyes. Although the photograph was grainy, Ayda recognised in her father a pose she often adopted, and recognised herself in one of her sisters. With wobbling fingers, she wrote their names and addresses in her address book and started to think about what she would write to them all. Her prayers had been answered. She had a family.

CHAPTER 39

Ayda would forever be grateful to Mabel for the part she had played in reuniting her with her family and they soon became firm friends. A few months after Mabel gave birth to her baby girl, Ava, she invited Ayda and Carl on a trip to the country.

'That's so kind of you, Mabel. Where did you have in mind?'

Mabel swaddled baby Ava expertly, then turned to Ayda. 'Well, you see, Cyril's just picked up a new Crossley motor. Nice big family car, it is, and he's just itching to take it out. His parents haven't met our little Ava yet, so I thought a trip to visit them would be just the thing. We could make a weekend of it, if you like?'

Ayda smiled. 'I think that's a wonderful idea, but you still haven't told me where they live.'

'Oxfordshire. In a little village called Middleton Stoney, near Bicester. Ever so quiet and picturesque. We were thinking of going next weekend?'

'Sounds perfect.'

Mabel beamed. 'That's settled then. Next Saturday it is!'

As the Crossley purred along, green fields and meadows swept past, and Ayda wondered how many times she must have followed this same route in the sky. Gentle vibrations from the big car's engine managed to lull the children to sleep, so the journey was peaceful. When they arrived, Mabel's in-laws fussed over their new granddaughter while Cyril, tired by the drive, settled into a comfy chair with his pipe.

Ayda was soon on her feet. 'Would anyone mind if I went for a stroll? The village looks so pretty, and I'd like to get my bearings if that's okay?'

Polworth House on the Old Commander Estate was well marked. Ayda had noticed the signs directing to it on their drive up. After a brisk walk east of two miles, she arrived on the outskirts of Bicester village. Passing a lake and some parkland, Ayda then moved up a winding drive, arriving at an impressive sandy-coloured Victorian house complete with clocktower.

A collection of cars and various tools were stored at its side, making the grounds appear more like a junkyard than a formal garden. A familiar smell filled the air. The fumes of fuel and oil made her nose wrinkle. Instinctively, Ayda looked around for aeroplanes. There were none. But something else caught her eye. A trio of white sheds stood before her, a hammering noise of metal on metal emanating from the middle shed.

As Ayda moved towards it, an engine fired up and clouds of blue smoke were pumped into her face by way of a greeting. She coughed and the hammering stopped. When the mist cleared, a face was staring at her. A face that hadn't changed much over the years.

'Goodness gracious, Ayda! Is it really you?' Thomas Shuttleby asked. 'I thought for a minute you were a ghost through all that smoke.'

'Hello, Thomas. Yes, it is me. I'm just passing through the area, and couldn't pass up the chance to see you.' She looked around. Engines lay piled in the corner coated in grease and oil, and several half-constructed car chassis were strewn across the floor. 'This all looks familiar.'

Thomas smiled weakly, wiping his hands on an oily cloth. 'I must apologise for the mess. I never mean to coat everything in muck and oil, but it's probably just the way I work.'

Ayda shrugged. 'Please don't mind me. It's refreshing, really, especially after being cooped up in an office.'

Thomas shoved his hands into his pockets. 'Now that does surprise me, Ayda. I thought you didn't enjoy typing and office work.'

'You're right, I don't, but I have a little boy to look after, and taking off in an aeroplane doesn't go terribly well with motherhood.'

'I see.'

'Well, what about you, Thomas?'

'Me? No, no. Well, at least not yet. I'm getting married at the end of the year, so who knows after then?'

'Congratulations!'

'Thank you. And what about you? Is there a husband, a father for your little boy?' Thomas glanced at Ayda's face. 'Let me guess. Another airman?'

Ayda nodded, not trusting her voice.

'Oh, Ayda, I am sorry.'

She looked around, examining the shed more closely, ready to change the subject. 'There are no planes here, so I see you've stuck to your promise of staying on terra firma.'

'I'm afraid so. With so many of my friends ending up like Adam, I thought why should I bother anymore. Besides, I do like cars.'

'But what have you done with your collection of planes? I can't believe there's nothing here, not even a strut or a prop shaft.'

'I didn't have the heart to get them from the Bound estate. Nasty man that Lord Granville. Didn't have the fight in me anymore. He's probably dismantled them by now or set fire to them, who knows?'

Ayda looked away, remembering Granville's cruelty. 'Yes, well, he always was a bad egg.'

Thomas nodded. 'But I heard he got his just deserts. Both legs blown off at an explosion in the Lochnagar crater — you know, the Glory Hole near La Boisselle. Couldn't have happened to a nicer chap, eh?'

Despite her intense dislike of Adam's brother, the news didn't fill Ayda with glee. The war had ruined enough lives.

Thomas handed her a piece of paper and a pen. 'Can you write down your address? I'll send you an invitation to the wedding.'

'I'd like that very much.' Ayda quickly wrote down her telephone number and address. She looked up. 'I've got something for you too.' Opening her coat, she removed a torn and faded envelope and handed it to Thomas. 'Your plans. For the Shuttlebound 11. Think about it please, Thomas. I know you want nothing to do with flying now, but in time that might change — maybe even for me. Just remember all those designers, all those airmen who died and will never get the chance to build or fly their dreams again. I'm sure Adam would have wanted you to.'

Reluctantly, Thomas took the envelope.

'Thank you, Thomas. That means a lot. Now I'd better be getting back to my son. It's been lovely to see you again.'

Thomas held out his hand. 'To friendship.'

Ayda smiled. 'To old friends.'

As she walked back to Mabel and her family, Ayda felt a warm glow inside her. Her close circle was expanding, with new and old friends, and family to get to know. Hopefully she and Carl would never be lonely again.

CHAPTER 40

Ayda was becoming tired of her job at *Nature* magazine. Working in admin had never appealed to her and she longed for the days of working with machines or helping with scientific discoveries. Her resolve not to think about flying was wavering, too. The turning point came when she noticed a full colour poster for the Bournemouth Flying Meeting pinned to the *Nature* magazine's office noticeboard. A tall woman stood in front of a sturdy, boxy bi-plane. The plane was an S.E.5a, and the woman standing in front of it looked proud and confident. Ayda felt sick. As Britain's first female dispatch pilot, what had *she* done?

Here was a woman, happy, fulfilled, following her dreams — like she had. Of all people, she should appreciate the woman's achievement and be happy for her, but all she could feel was envy.

The following day, Cameron Muir called her up.

'You've been looking a little lacklustre these days, Ayda, as if your heart isn't in it. So I've come up with a plan which I think might prove helpful. Before you say no, just hear me out. I have arranged a little job for you, my girl — it will also help out a friend in need. Young pilot, name of Christopher Parkes. I met him the other night and he said he is in desperate need of another flying instructor to help out. I told him I knew just the person. He works at a flying school on the Edgware/Kingsbury border.'

'You mean Stag Lane Aerodrome?' Ayda asked.

'You've heard of it? Christopher's a pleasant chap, but he's working there all hours, teaching. He'd like to gain his commercial licence but hasn't the time, and there's a huge waiting list of would-be pilots, so I've told him I know someone who could help. So, Ayda... What do you say?'

Though her first impulse was to say no, Ayda knew it was time to get back in the air. With no excuses at the ready, she offered no resistance. Already feeling the rush of wind, of adrenaline, she began to feel giddy.

'Yes, I'll do it,' she whispered.

The London Flying School at Stag Lane Aerodrome consisted of four hangars and, nestled next to several other schools, it offered flying lessons for a very competitive thirty shillings. When Ayda arrived she noticed that the school's two De Havilland Moths looked overworked, but she immediately felt at home. A group of male pilots, hands in pockets, had gathered round for an inspection — of her. Sadly, Ayda was all too familiar with this type of behaviour, realising some things hadn't changed in ten years. Stepping forwards, the largest of the group, a swaggering chump of a man, cocked his head to the side.

'Can you actually fly, Miss?'

Ayda felt herself pulled back in time — to Hendon, trying to get her ticket — to Farnborough, and its sniggering assessor. But the difference now was stark: she was no longer an inexperienced young woman of twenty. 'Yes, I can, and probably better than any of you. Just watch and see.'

Christopher Parkes was waiting for her on the concrete next to a small boxy plane. The London Aero Club painted its planes yellow, making the Gypsy Moth more canary than moth, but Ayda didn't care.

'Everyone's impressed with the Moth's folding wings, saves so much space in the hangars.' A greasy hand extended towards her. 'I'm Christopher. It's good to meet you at last, Mrs Bound. And I'm very grateful to have you on board.'

'Lovely to meet you, Christopher, but do call me Ayda.'

Taking to the air felt like meeting up with an old friend. She flooded the Moth's carburettors, then closed its throttle, before shouting, 'Contact!'. The propeller swung round as the little plane throbbed to life. Inside, the Moth's cockpit felt narrow, cramped and slightly boxed in with its wings directly above her head, and the visibility as she taxied along was not as good as she would have liked.

With only two ailerons, the Moth didn't roll or climb as fast as an S.E.5a, but she didn't care. It was light and responsive, and she was finally flying. Ayda kicked the rudder for all it was worth, stood the little plane on its tail, kicked the rudder again, finding that it went right over into a loop, which it seemed to like to do. Letting out a delighted whoop, she knew she hadn't had so much fun in ages. On landing her head finally cleared; she understood the true meaning of the saying 'like a breath of fresh air'.

As she taxied along, a tall dark-haired woman gave her a shy wave. Christopher had mentioned that the young woman worked nearby and often sat watching the flights during her lunch hour. When Ayda read through her September list she wondered if the woman's name might be on it. Since her arrival the school had become busier still, with her lessons proving so popular that she was booked up for the next two years. And many of the names on her lists were female: Grace Pearce, Camilla Foxton, Jacinta O'Leary and Amy Johnson were some of the ones in the next cohort.

After working there for a few months Christopher told Ayda there was someone who wanted to meet her.

'His name is Samuel Cooper. He used to run the stores here, clean the toilets and such stuff. But he hasn't been around much lately, as his health isn't that good, but when he found out you were an instructor here, he asked me to introduce you.'

'Why does he want to meet me?'

Christopher shrugged. 'He didn't say.'

Samuel Cooper had asked to meet Ayda one night after work. The aerodrome was slightly chilly that evening and the crisp breeze that swept across the tarmac runways carried with it the buzz of planes being put to bed in their hangars. An ultramarine sky hung above showcasing a kaleidoscope of colours as she walked past the last hangar to a small, lonely building. Weatherboarded and pokey, the storeroom at the Flying School was the allotted meeting place, and its freshly painted door creaked when Ayda pushed it open.

An Aladdin's cave awaited her with a heady mix of carbolic, polish and oil. Filled with an assortment of objects, Ayda took it all in: an old wind sock, three broken radio transmitters, brushes of all shapes and sizes on a wall festooned with tattered flying coats from a different era, and as her fingertips landed on the hardened leather a pang of nostalgia caught her unaware. Just then a clanging noise made her look across towards a window at the far side.

The sun was fading fast now throwing the last of its colours from the sky as a dying ray of light pierced the window, framing the outline of a man clutching a broom. Moving closer, Ayda noticed sandy hair with flecks of grey, and red, blistered bald patches before a spasm suddenly gripped the man's leg, making him stagger towards a table. The man looked up and Ayda gasped.

Ayda hadn't realised how much Carl resembled his father until then: his build, the shape of his head — and eyes of the deepest blue that penetrated through to the soul.

Time immediately stopped. How could Rick be here? She ran to him, burying herself in his chest, not looking up lest he should disappear. The tears came like a torrent, all those years of grief released. And when she could finally talk, she asked only one question. How?

A raspier, throatier sound came from Rick than she remembered, though the rich, sing-song voice was still there. Wiping his eyes, he began.

'Some might say, I was one of the lucky ones — others not, but I know I owe you an explanation. Shame, disgust, grief and pain were my companions on that last flight — 3rd October 1918 … and they still haunt me to this day.' The shaking began again and he paused, waiting for it to subside. 'By all accounts, I should have died, indeed, I had intended to, but in the heat of it all, my hand slipped on my revolver and I was somehow spared. Then I felt myself being pulled from the burning wreckage as my S.E.5a submerged into a reservoir. My uniform and identity tags were destroyed by the fire.'

Rick took a deep breath through his dry lips, clinging hard to the table.

'I was treated for severe burns at Hôpital Saint-Louis in Paris, then transferred to a military hospital in Clamart where I remained for months. By then, the war had ended — and so had my life as Major Rick Randal, who I left behind in the burning wreck of his sinking plane. I reinvented myself as Second Lieutenant Samuel Cooper, and as the war had ended, few questions were asked. I was free to leave my guilt and grief behind, but I began to crave home in a way I didn't think possible — and you, Ayda, thinking that perhaps one day I might pluck up the courage to return — but these…' Rick stared at the charred remains of his hands. 'I couldn't do it. Fearing rejection, I couldn't make myself return to you — some hero, eh? So, eventually, I came here — to something I knew and loved, shying away from people but still hoping one day it might lead to you. And it did. I'm so sorry Ayda, I wanted to come back to you, but I have suffered. Suffered terribly. And I didn't know how.'

'But your grave, Rick. We visited.'

'Some other poor sod, I should imagine. Plenty to choose from on that day.'

Ayda took him in her arms again. She was sad at the time they had lost, but how could she be angry at the broken man standing in front of her? He was here now, he had returned to her, and that was all that mattered.

Ayda took Rick home to meet Carl. Carl gave his father's clawed hand a tiny squeeze, and tears flowed down Rick's cheeks.

Carl shrank back a little, worried, but his eyes never left his father's — deep blue on deep blue, a shy smile starting on his upturned face, and Rick reached across to gently stroke his face.

'Don't be afraid son, even heroes burn.'

Ayda let out a long breath she hadn't realised she had been holding. The three of them were finally together.

'Look, just forget Rick Randal ever existed,' Rick said to Ayda. 'He died along with his plane, so, just let him rest, all right? No one will ask any questions.'

Six months later, still not believing her luck, Ayda became Mrs Samuel Cooper, leading as quiet a life as possible with the man she loved and thought lost, the little things between them telling their story: Rick's eyes never leaving hers, Ayda always touching him to make sure he was real. Rick kept his position as janitor, though rarely accompanied his wife to Stag Lane on her instructor days, still preferring the cover of darkness and shadows, retreating more into Samuel Cooper. And looking up at the sky, she remembered Adam and she thanked the stars he had always been fascinated by for guiding her back to flying, and reuniting her with Rick.

The sky was vast, impenetrable, the place where she felt most at home, but now it had no more secrets left to tell.

HISTORICAL NOTES

In writing *Secrets in the Sky* I have tried my best to be historically and factually accurate. But, as you can appreciate, the history of the First World War is vast, and the facts as they come to light can vary slightly over time. With that said, most of the main characters are based on real people who fought, in particular Adam Bound and Rick Randal, who were inspired by real aces of the period. My main character, Ayda, is a mixture of several strong women and entirely fictional.

Occasionally, it was necessary to deviate from the facts. For instance, when researching a suitable venue for my scientific meeting in October 1913, I couldn't find one available at Elstree. I had read about the history of Elstree Film Studios, which despite its name was in nearby Borehamwood, but the studios' predecessor was called Neptune Studios, which opened in January 1914. It was a modern studio dedicated to the science of film-making, perfect for a meeting of scientific minds! The timing was out by three months, but in October 1913, I reasoned, the building would probably have been near completion, so, for the purposes of this book, I called it Neptune Hall. After all, it wasn't a studio yet.

The only other factual departure is in the squadrons' unit numbers. Royal Flying Corps Squadrons were always numbered with no letters, unlike my fictitious 39a and 65a. The reason for this is so that no one can say there was no such person in 39 or 65 Squadrons at that time.

As a librarian and lover of books old and new, I have enjoyed getting lost in the characters and period of the First World War, although writing this book has, at times, been a labour of love. Some of the books used for research include: *Ace with One Eye: The Story of 'Mick' Mannock VC* by Frederick Oughton and Commander Vernon Smyth, James McCudden's *Five Years in the Royal Flying Corps*, *Wings over the Somme* by Wing Commander Gwilym H. Lewis D.F.C., and *An Airman's Wife* by Aimée McHardy. The rest of my research was conducted through visits to Belgium and northern France and from articles online.

A NOTE TO THE READER

Dear Reader,

Thank you for taking the time to read *Secrets in the Sky*, which I hope you enjoyed. The inspiration for this book came quite by chance, when I was just a teenager talking to a lady in her mid-eighties. Having politely listened to her for over an hour, I was about to make my excuses, when she began talking about the First World War and her long-lost fiancé. 'Was he in the trenches?' I asked. 'Oh no,' she replied, with much pride and a glint in her eye. 'Not at all — in fact, he was an aviator.'

Two hours later, it had turned dark outside and I had learnt that given half the chance, this dear old lady would have loved to have flown too. It was then that the first imaginings of Ayda de Corsi's character stirred in my mind. Unfortunately, I never saw the lady again. Over the years, I thought of her often, particularly when, about twenty-five years later, I found myself heading to France on a ferry, feeling nauseous and wishing I could fly. Ayda's character stirred again in my head, as did the elderly lady's stories, which were still tucked away there. By then, I felt a real desire to find out more about the First World War, and its forgotten airmen.

When writing an historical novel, much research is necessary and one can easily become obsessed. Who were these airmen who went to war in skeletal crafts with bicycle tyres? It helped that I became a librarian; it also helped visiting the immaculately maintained Commonwealth War Graves Commission (CWGC) cemeteries of Belgium and northern France, which were both peaceful and interesting. I learned about the aces, the VCs, but also about those airmen who were sent to war with a mere nine hours' flying time, and, along with countless others, made the ultimate sacrifice.

After reading their brave stories the characters of Adam Bound, Thomas Shuttleby and of course, Rick Randal, came easily! But all the time there was always Ayda: a capable, incredibly talented woman (of which there were many), a mixture of Ada Lovelace and Amy Johnson, who lived at a time when women did *not* engage in warfare.

Well, what if a woman had a civilian role like those in the Air Transport Auxiliary (ATA) of the Second World War, I reasoned, and what if that role was secret? And suddenly there was Ayda, and the rest, as they say, is history! Over the years, people have always asked me the same question: *Did people really fly in the First World War?* Well, now you know the answer!

Reviews by readers these days are integral to a book's success, so if you enjoyed Ayda's tale I would be very grateful if you could spare a minute to post a review on **Amazon** and **Goodreads**. I love hearing from readers, and you can talk with me **on Twitter** and follow my author page **on Facebook**.

Suzanne Parsons

Printed in Great Britain
by Amazon

49074013R00139